Brentwood Public Library
Brentwood, NY 11717

P9-DMU-280

8/19

SUPER POTATO

#3 SUPER POTATO'S MEGA TIME-TRAVEL ADVENTURE

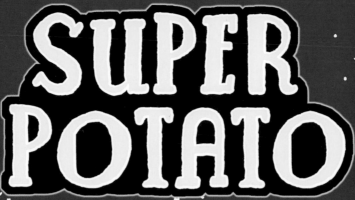

ARTUR LAPERLA

Graphic Universe™ • Minneapolis

Story and illustrations by Artur Laperla
Translation by Norwyn MacTíre

First American edition published in 2019 by Graphic Universe™

Copyright © 2014 by Artur Laperla and Bang. Ediciones. Published by arrangement with Garbuix Agency.

English translation copyright © 2019 by Lerner Publishing Group, Inc.

Graphic Universe™ is a trademark of Lerner Publishing Group, Inc.

All US rights reserved. No part of this book may be reproduced, stored in a retrieval system, or transmitted in any form or by any means—electronic, mechanical, photocopying, recording, or otherwise—without the prior written permission of Lerner Publishing Group, Inc., except for the inclusion of brief quotations in an acknowledged review.

Graphic Universe™
A division of Lerner Publishing Group, Inc.
241 First Avenue North
Minneapolis, MN 55401 USA

For reading levels and more information, look up this title at www.lernerbooks.com.

Main body text set in CCWildWords 8.5/10. Typeface provided by Comicraft.

Library of Congress Cataloging-in-Publication Data

Names: Laperla (Artist) author, illustrator.
Title: Super Potato's mega time-travel adventure / Artur Laperla ; translation by
   Norwyn MacTíre.
Other titles: Super Patata. 3. English | Mega time-travel adventure
Description: First American edition. | Minneapolis : Graphic Universe, 2019. | Series: Super
   Potato ; book 3 | Originally published in Spanish: Barcelona : Bang Ediciones, 2014. |
   Summary: "Super Potato travels back in time in an effort to prevent his transformation
   from man into potato" —Provided by publisher.
Identifiers: LCCN 2018036038 (print) | LCCN 2018042006 (ebook) | ISBN 9781541561144 (eb pdf)
   | ISBN 9781512440232 (lb : alk. paper)
Subjects: LCSH: Graphic novels. | CYAC: Graphic novels. | Superheroes—Fiction. | Time
   travel—Fiction. | Potatoes—Fiction. | Humorous stories.
Classification: LCC PZ7.7.L367 (ebook) | LCC PZ7.7.L367 Sw 2019 (print) | DDC 741.5/973—dc23

LC record available at https://lccn.loc.gov/2018036038

Manufactured in the United States of America
1-42292-26142-10/22/2018

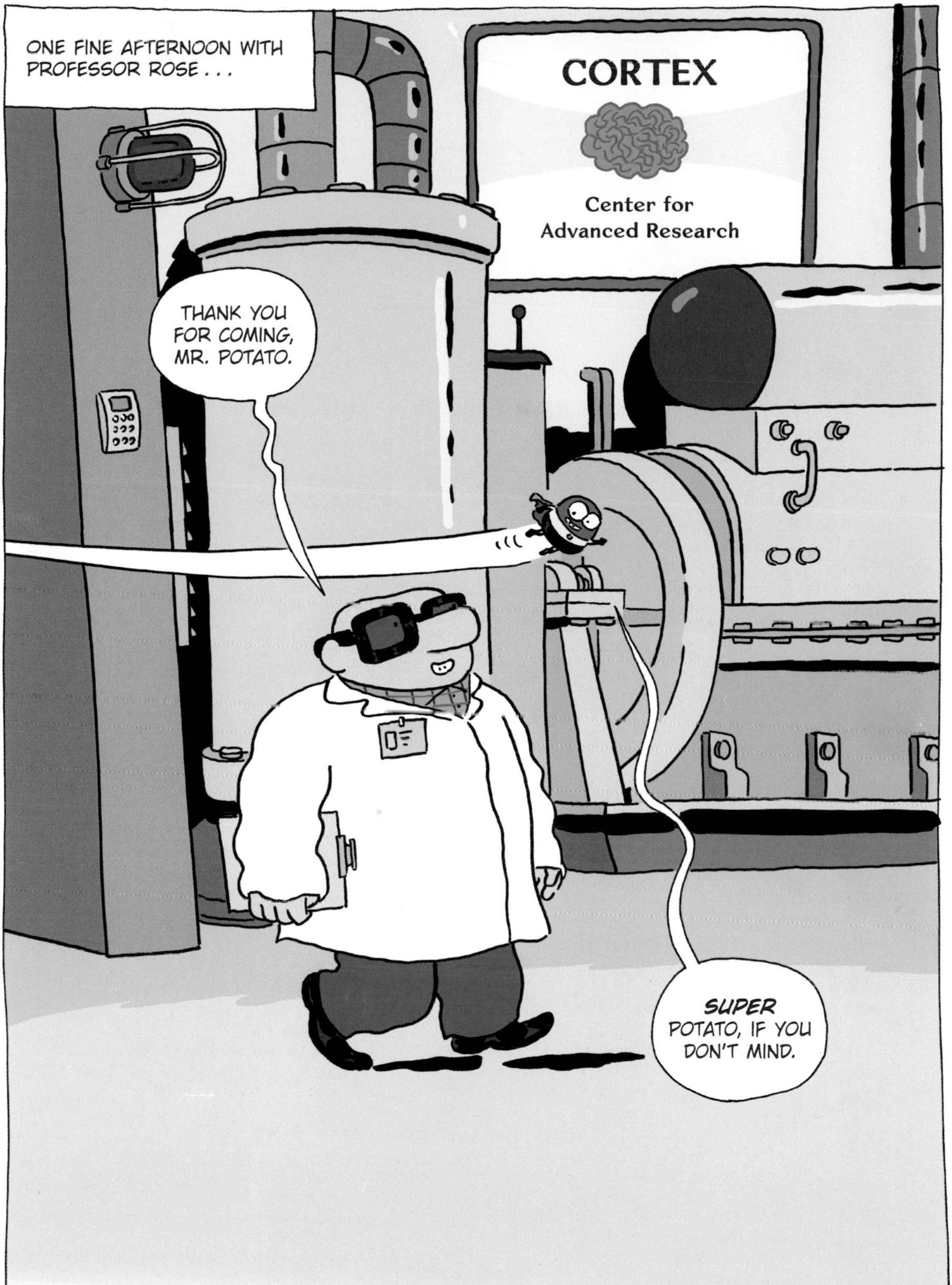
ONE FINE AFTERNOON WITH PROFESSOR ROSE . . .
CORTEX
Center for Advanced Research
THANK YOU FOR COMING, MR. POTATO.
SUPER POTATO, IF YOU DON'T MIND.

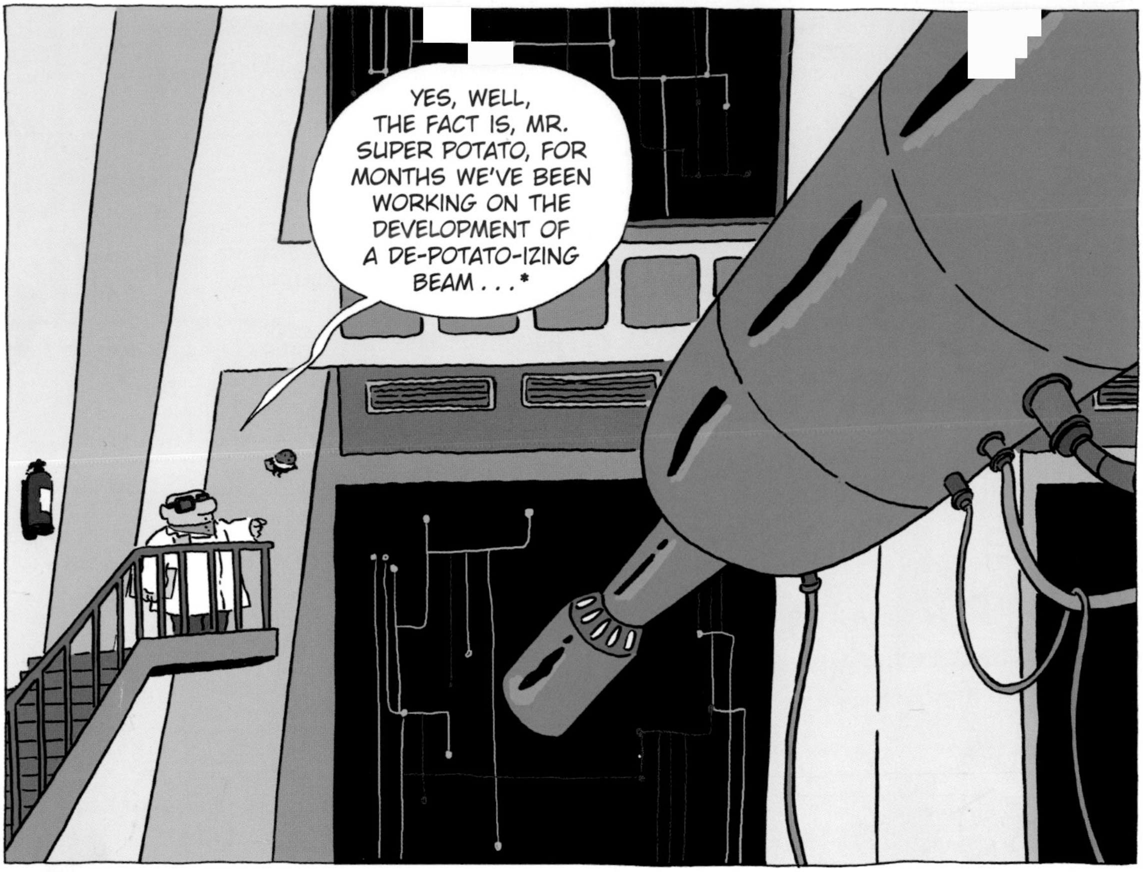
YES, WELL, THE FACT IS, MR. SUPER POTATO, FOR MONTHS WE'VE BEEN WORKING ON THE DEVELOPMENT OF A DE-POTATO-IZING BEAM . . .*

*IT'S TRUE! AS EVERYONE KNOWS (AND IF YOU DON'T, JUST READ THE FIRST BOOK IN THIS SERIES), SUPER POTATO IS REALLY SUPER MAX, TURNED INTO A TUBER BY THE POTATO-IZING BEAM OF THE EVIL DOCTOR MALEVOLENT.

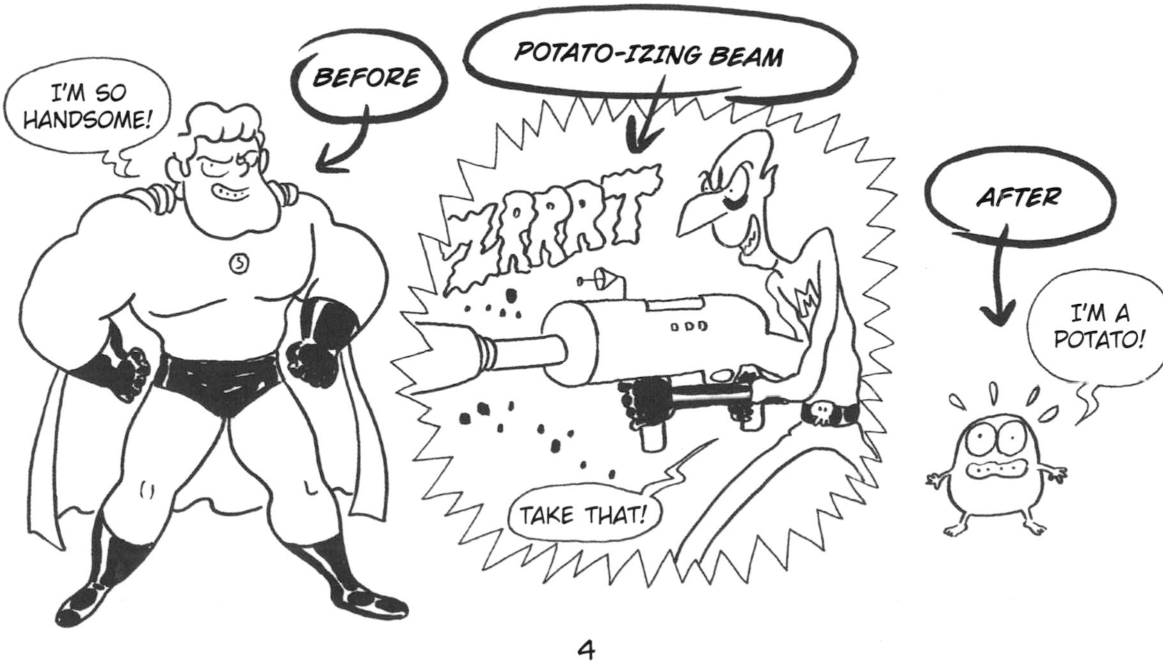
I'M SO HANDSOME!
BEFORE
POTATO-IZING BEAM
ZRRRT
TAKE THAT!
AFTER
I'M A POTATO!

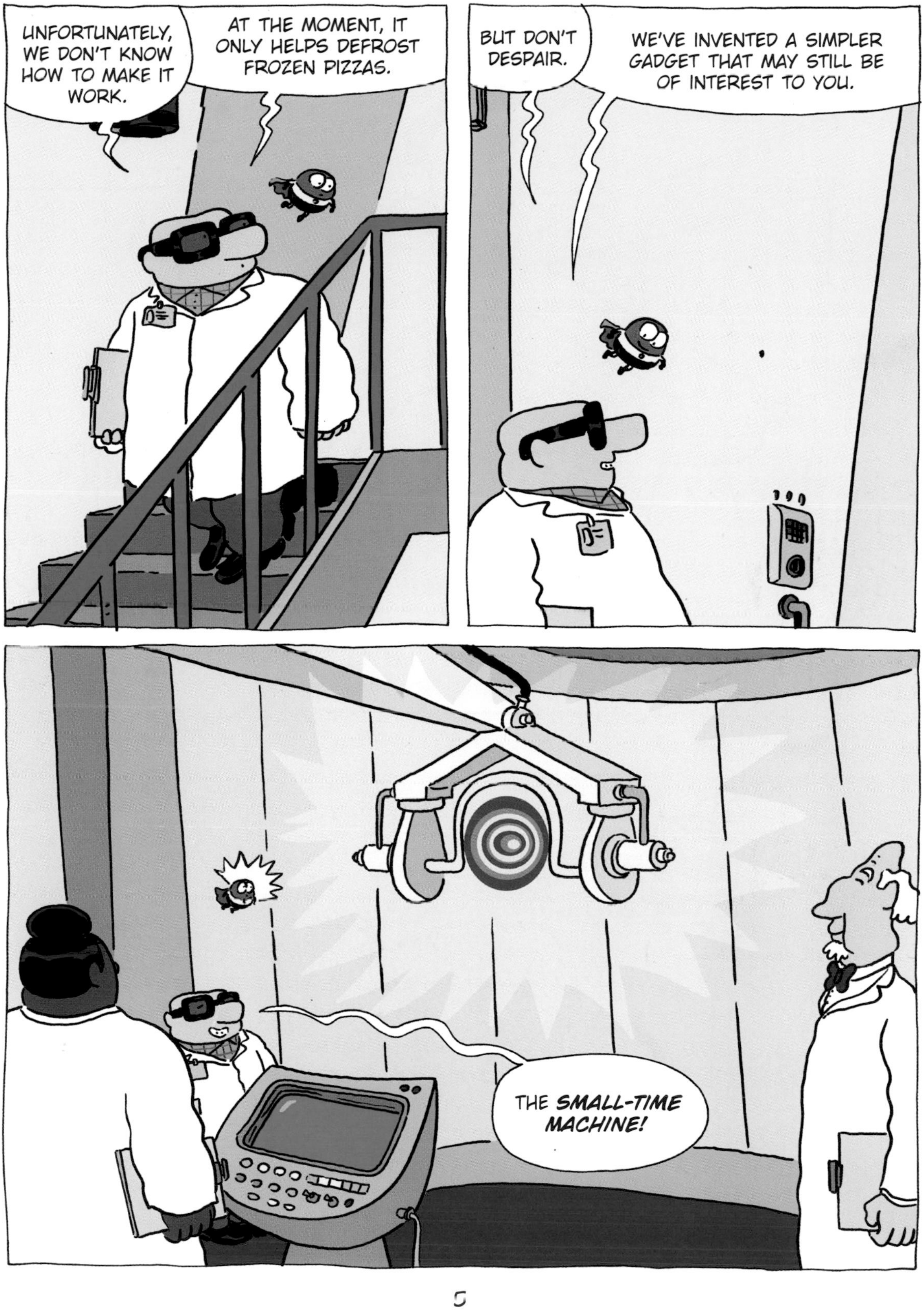
UNFORTUNATELY, WE DON'T KNOW HOW TO MAKE IT WORK.
AT THE MOMENT, IT ONLY HELPS DEFROST FROZEN PIZZAS.
BUT DON'T DESPAIR.
WE'VE INVENTED A SIMPLER GADGET THAT MAY STILL BE OF INTEREST TO YOU.
THE **SMALL-TIME MACHINE!**

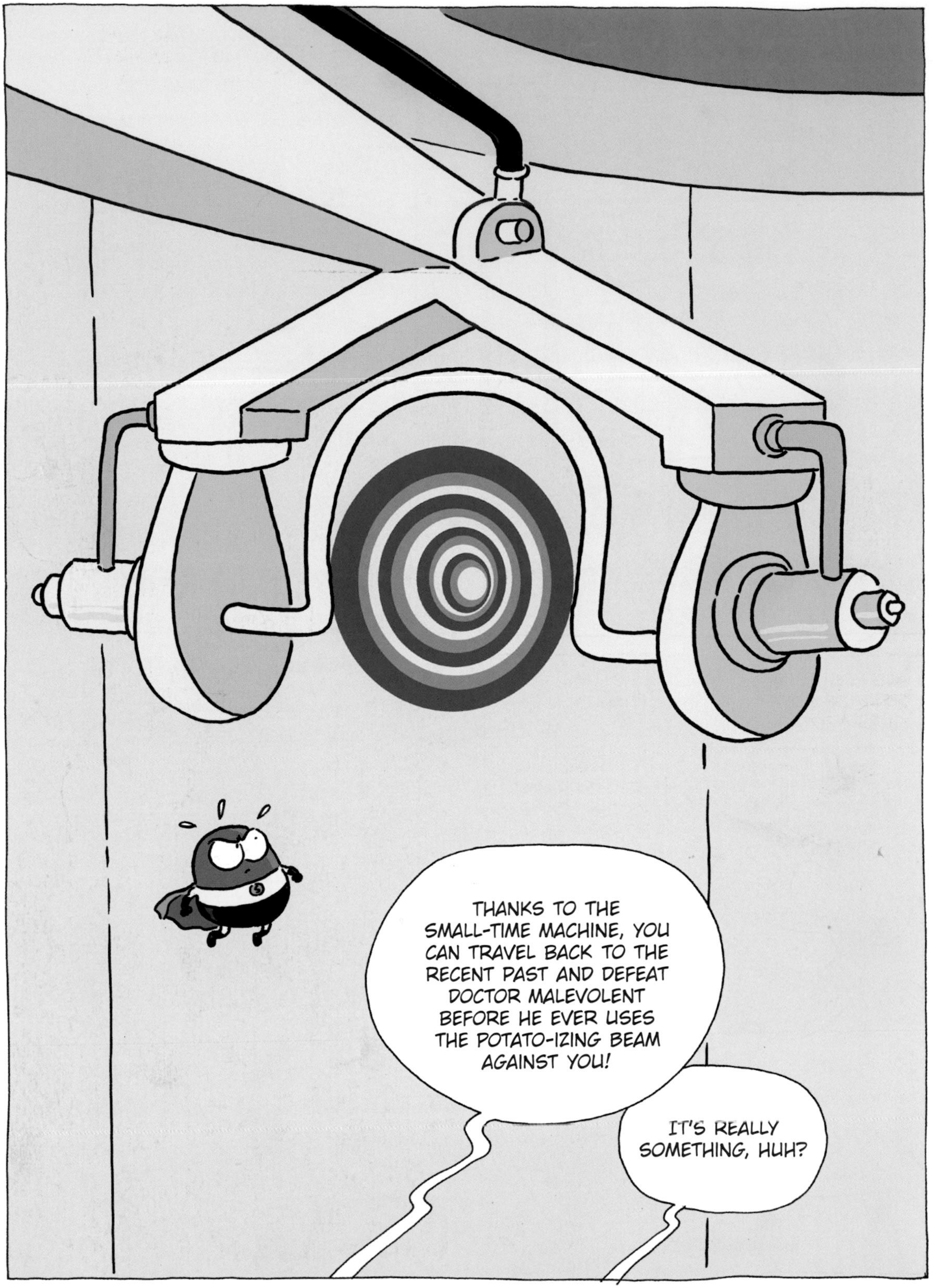
THANKS TO THE SMALL-TIME MACHINE, YOU CAN TRAVEL BACK TO THE RECENT PAST AND DEFEAT DOCTOR MALEVOLENT BEFORE HE EVER USES THE POTATO-IZING BEAM AGAINST YOU!
IT'S REALLY SOMETHING, HUH?

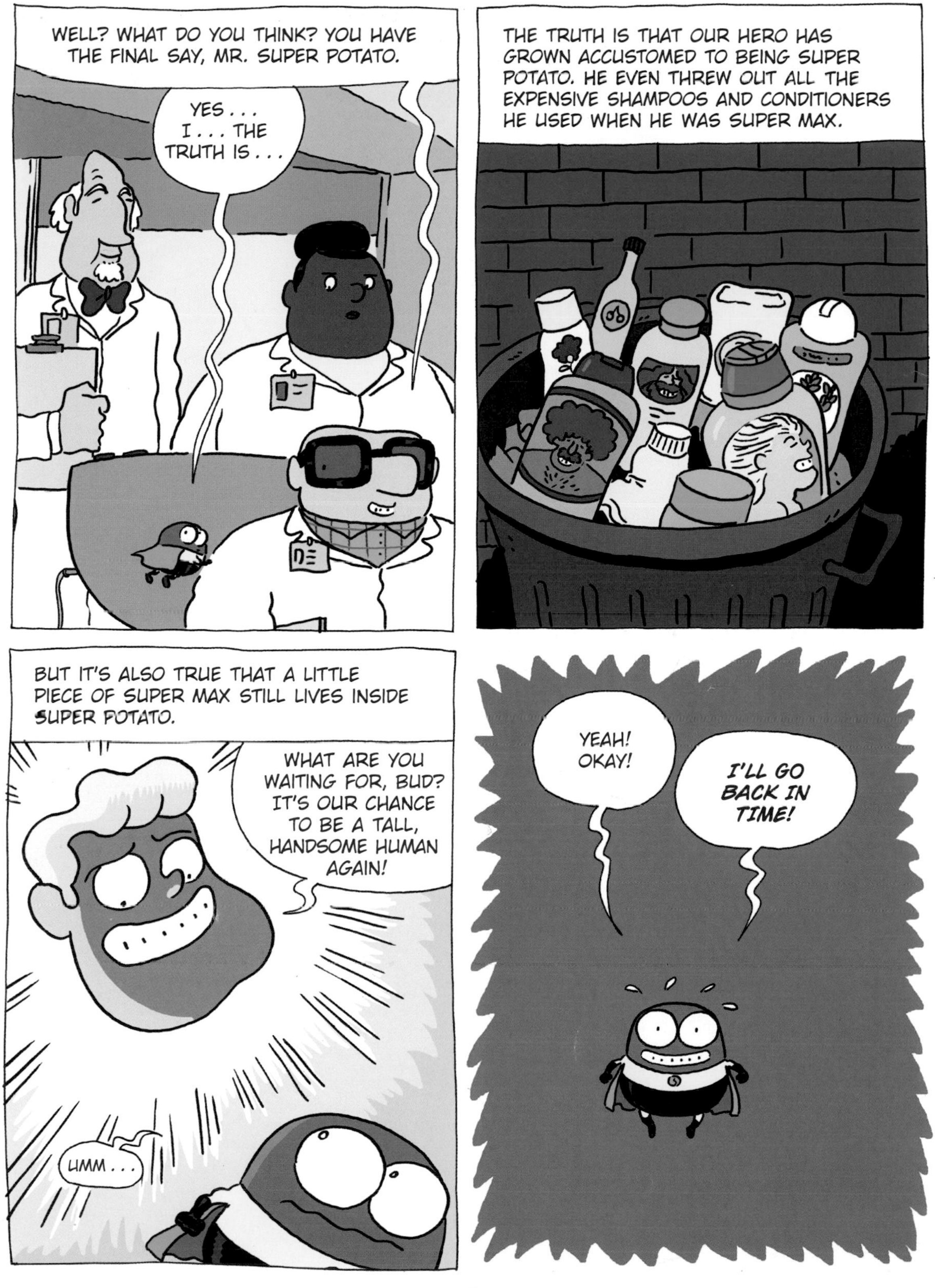
WELL? WHAT DO YOU THINK? YOU HAVE THE FINAL SAY, MR. SUPER POTATO.
YES . . . I . . . THE TRUTH IS . . .
THE TRUTH IS THAT OUR HERO HAS GROWN ACCUSTOMED TO BEING SUPER POTATO. HE EVEN THREW OUT ALL THE EXPENSIVE SHAMPOOS AND CONDITIONERS HE USED WHEN HE WAS SUPER MAX.
BUT IT'S ALSO TRUE THAT A LITTLE PIECE OF SUPER MAX STILL LIVES INSIDE SUPER POTATO.
WHAT ARE YOU WAITING FOR, BUD? IT'S OUR CHANCE TO BE A TALL, HANDSOME HUMAN AGAIN!
UMM . . .
YEAH! OKAY!
I'LL GO BACK IN TIME!

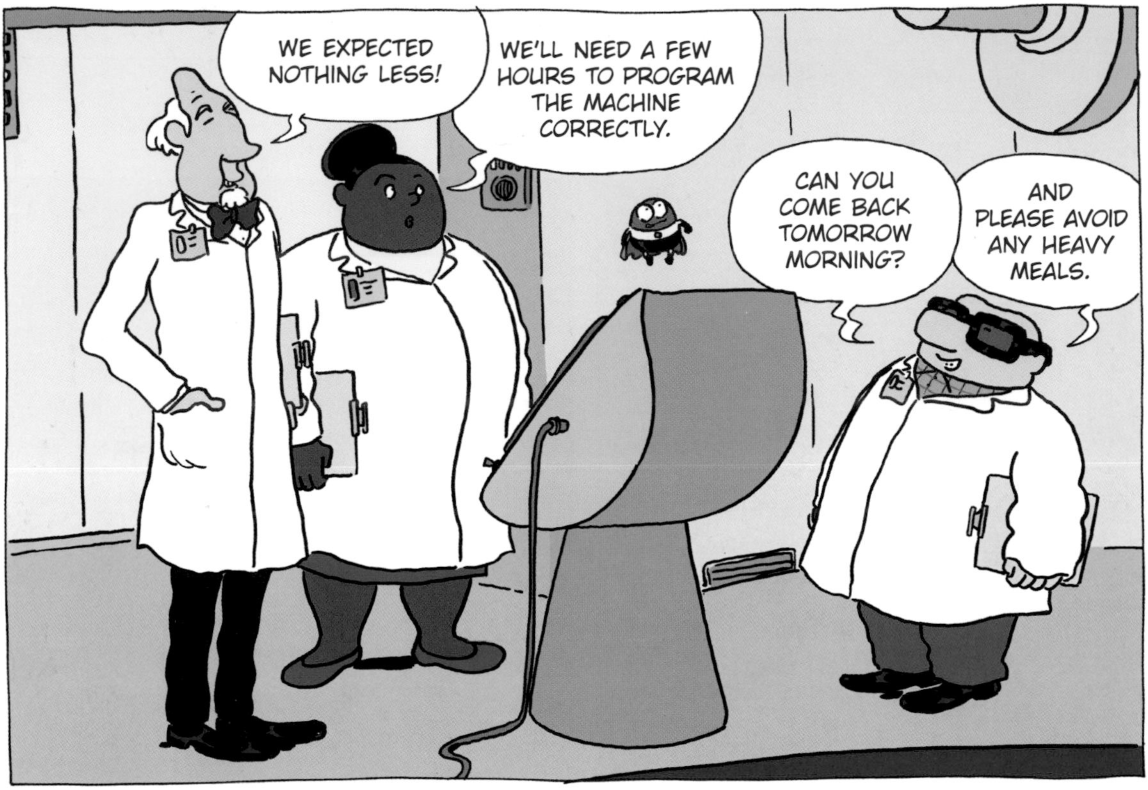
WE EXPECTED NOTHING LESS!
WE'LL NEED A FEW HOURS TO PROGRAM THE MACHINE CORRECTLY.
CAN YOU COME BACK TOMORROW MORNING?
AND PLEASE AVOID ANY HEAVY MEALS.

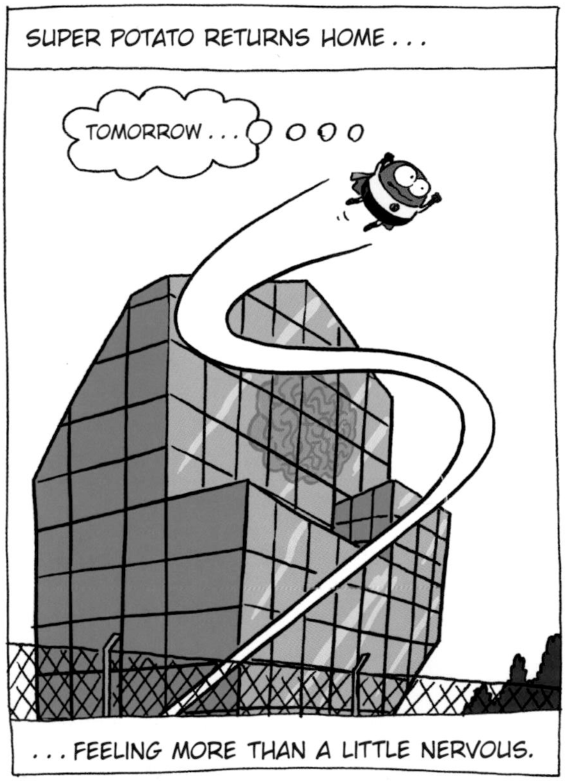
SUPER POTATO RETURNS HOME . . .
TOMORROW . . .
. . . FEELING MORE THAN A LITTLE NERVOUS.

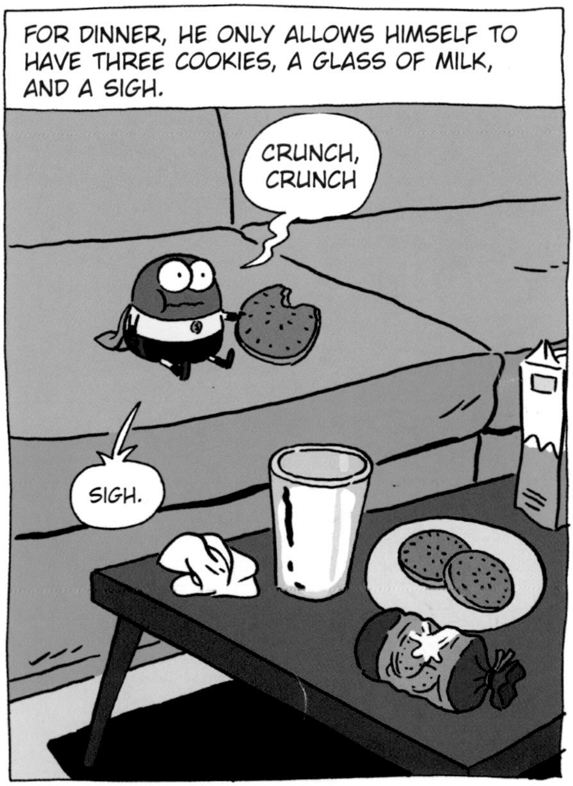
FOR DINNER, HE ONLY ALLOWS HIMSELF TO HAVE THREE COOKIES, A GLASS OF MILK, AND A SIGH.
CRUNCH, CRUNCH
SIGH.

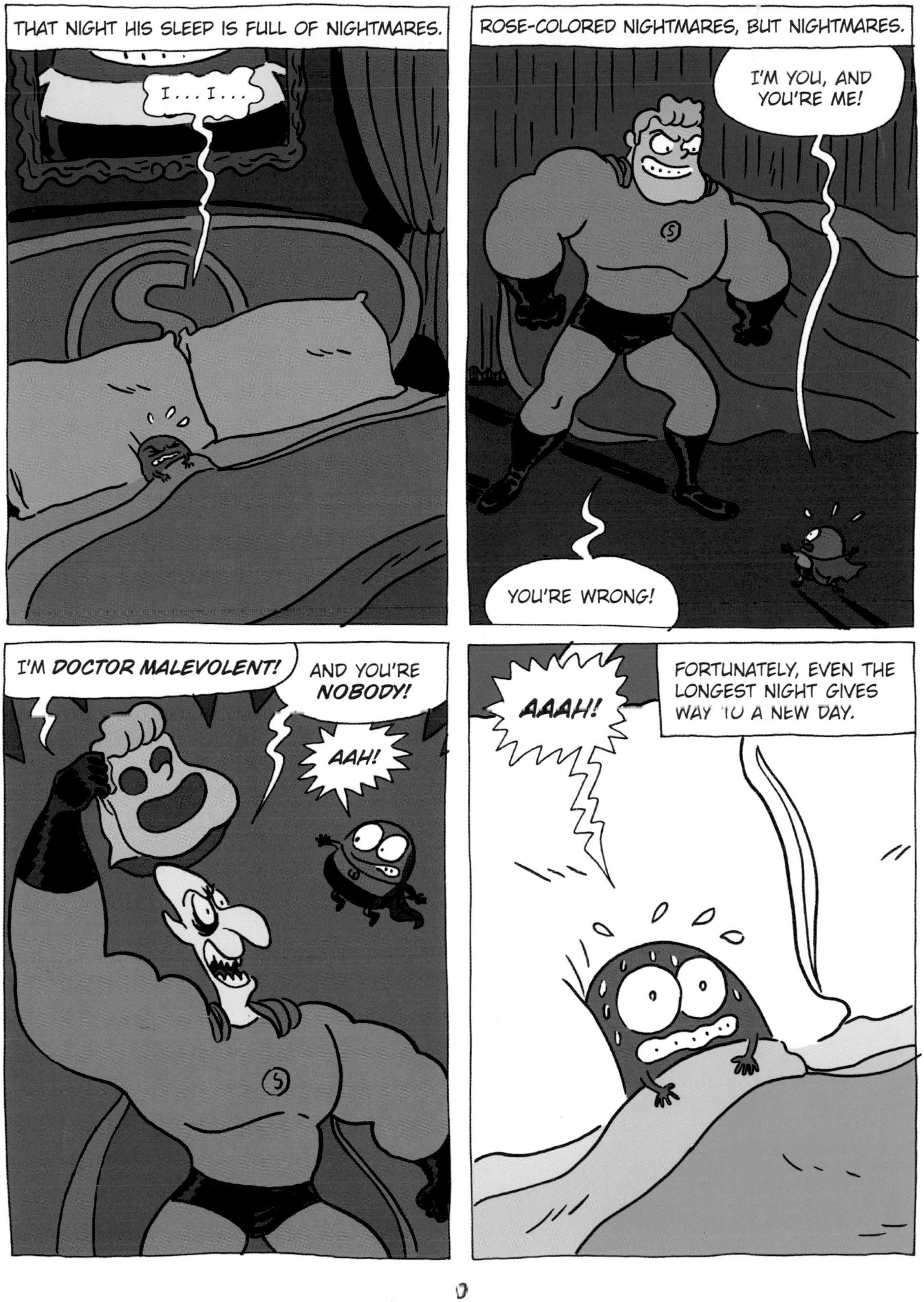
THAT NIGHT HIS SLEEP IS FULL OF NIGHTMARES.
I... I...
ROSE-COLORED NIGHTMARES, BUT NIGHTMARES.
I'M YOU, AND YOU'RE ME!
YOU'RE WRONG!
I'M DOCTOR MALEVOLENT!
AND YOU'RE NOBODY!
AAH!
AAAH!
FORTUNATELY, EVEN THE LONGEST NIGHT GIVES WAY TO A NEW DAY.

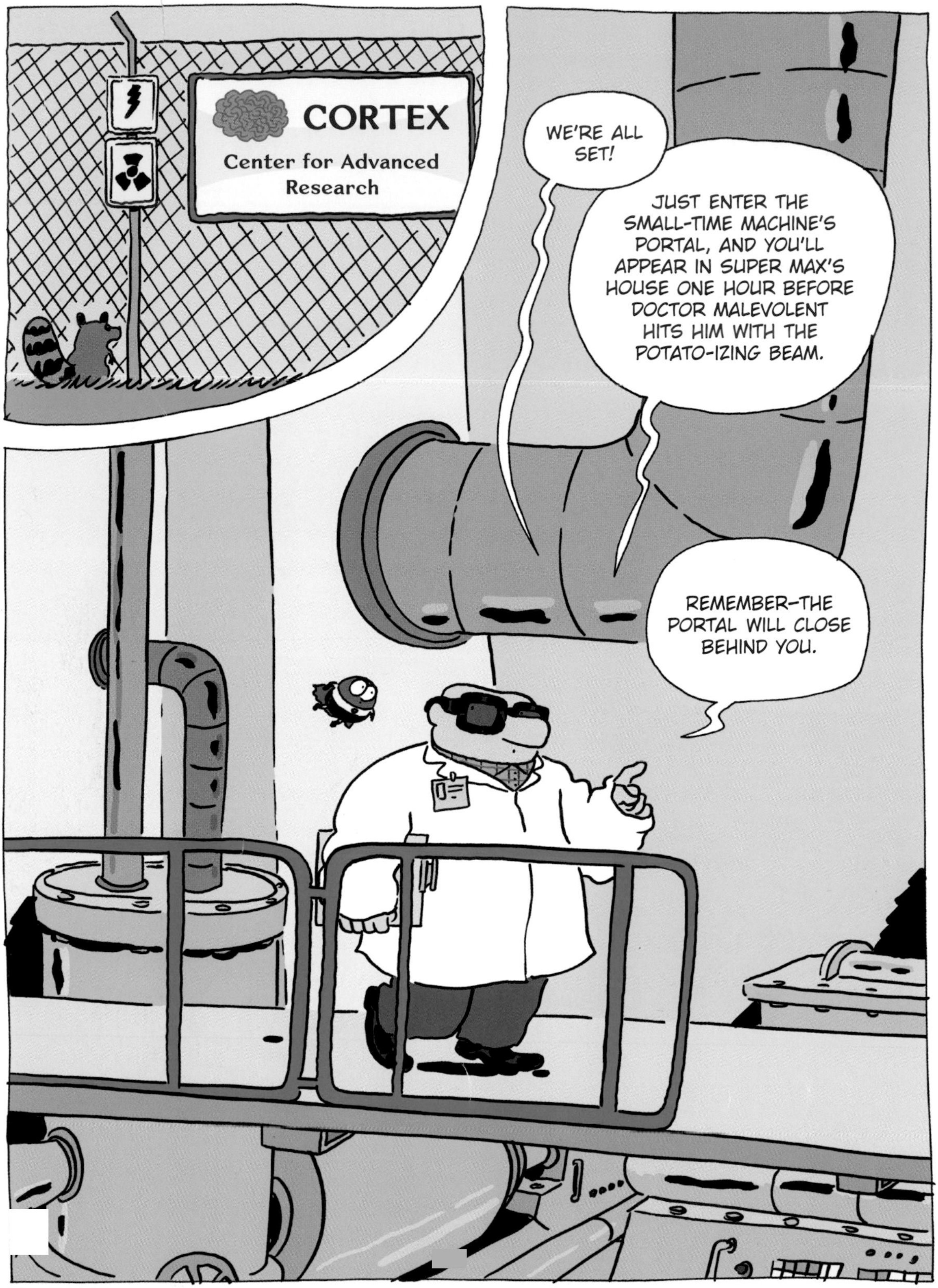
CORTEX
Center for Advanced Research
WE'RE ALL SET!
JUST ENTER THE SMALL-TIME MACHINE'S PORTAL, AND YOU'LL APPEAR IN SUPER MAX'S HOUSE ONE HOUR BEFORE DOCTOR MALEVOLENT HITS HIM WITH THE POTATO-IZING BEAM.
REMEMBER—THE PORTAL WILL CLOSE BEHIND YOU.

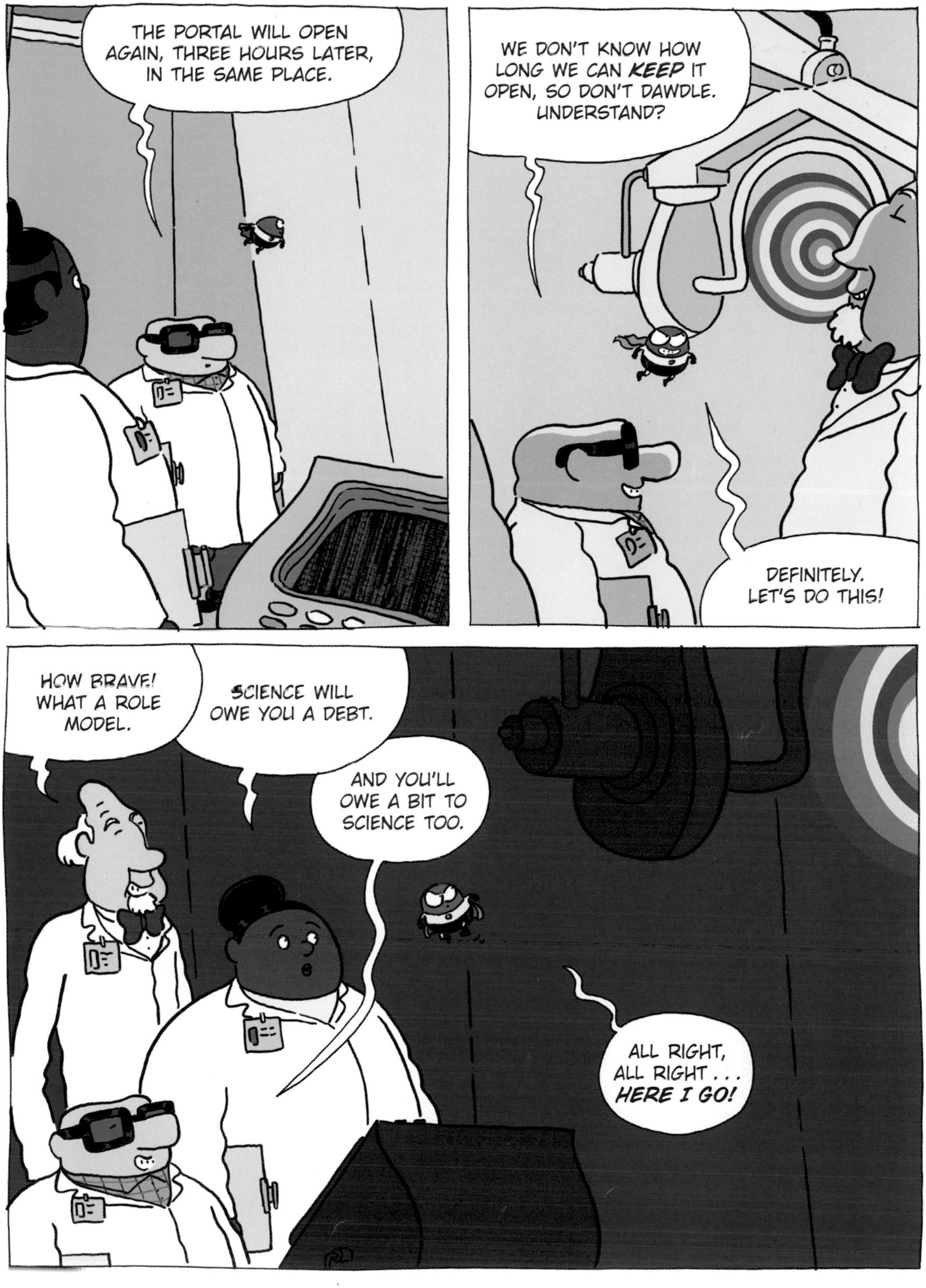
THE PORTAL WILL OPEN AGAIN, THREE HOURS LATER, IN THE SAME PLACE.
WE DON'T KNOW HOW LONG WE CAN *KEEP* IT OPEN, SO DON'T DAWDLE. UNDERSTAND?
DEFINITELY. LET'S DO THIS!
HOW BRAVE! WHAT A ROLE MODEL.
SCIENCE WILL OWE YOU A DEBT.
AND YOU'LL OWE A BIT TO SCIENCE TOO.
ALL RIGHT, ALL RIGHT . . . *HERE I GO!*

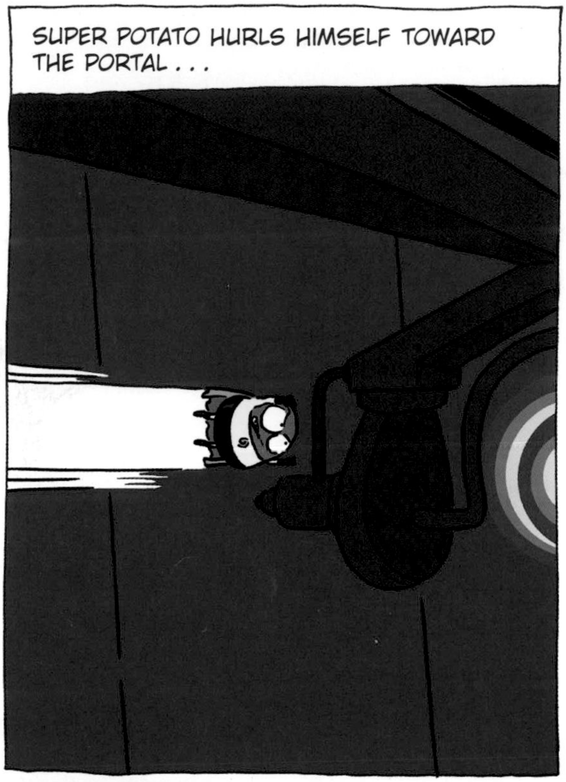
SUPER POTATO HURLS HIMSELF TOWARD THE PORTAL . . .

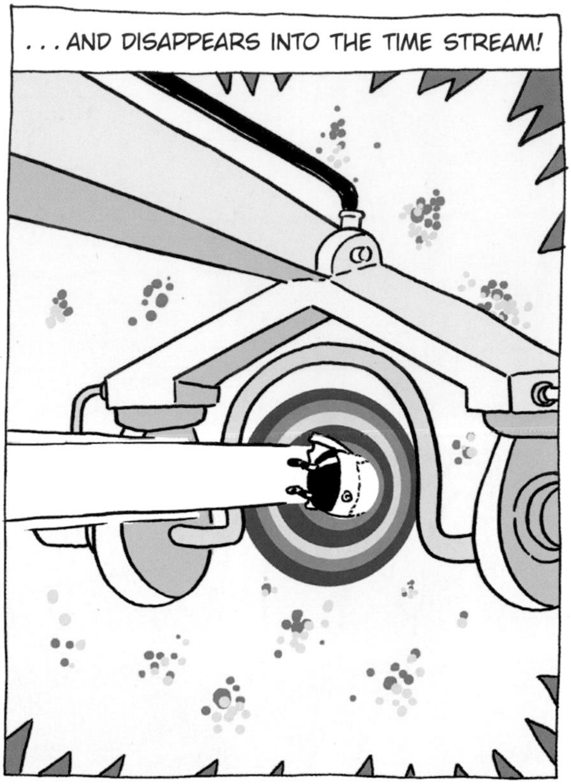
. . . AND DISAPPEARS INTO THE TIME STREAM!

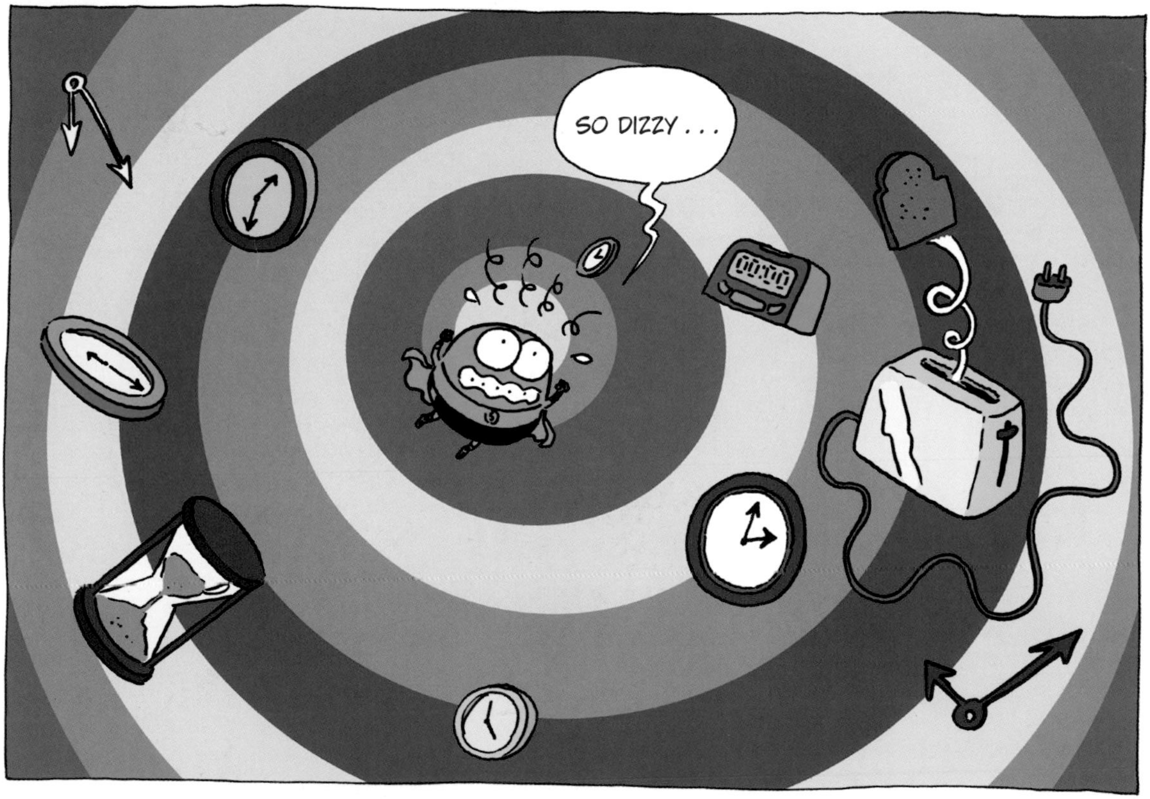
SO DIZZY . . .

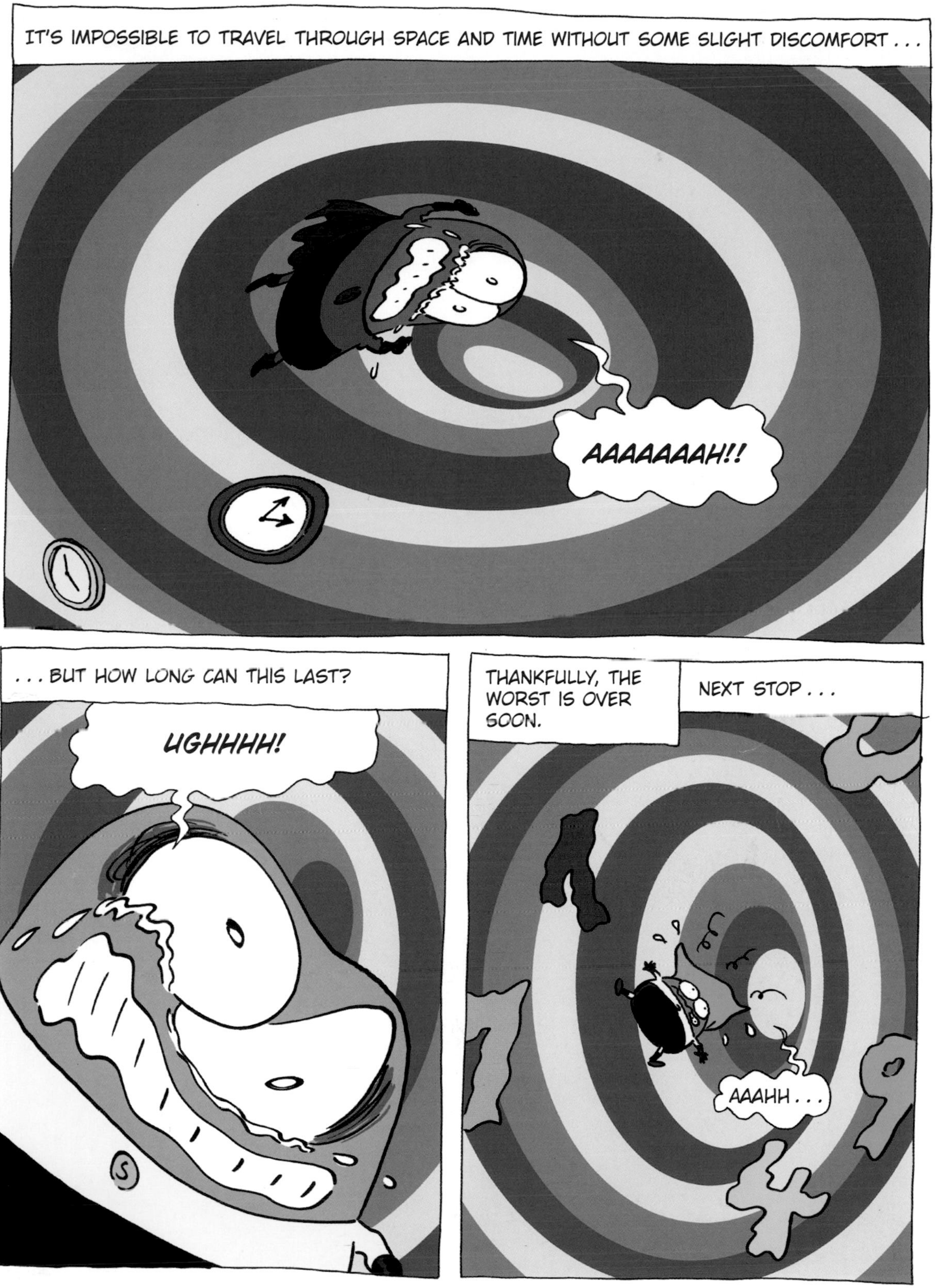
IT'S IMPOSSIBLE TO TRAVEL THROUGH SPACE AND TIME WITHOUT SOME SLIGHT DISCOMFORT . . .
AAAAAAAH!!
. . . BUT HOW LONG CAN THIS LAST?
UGHHHH!
THANKFULLY, THE WORST IS OVER SOON.
NEXT STOP . . .
AAAHH . . .

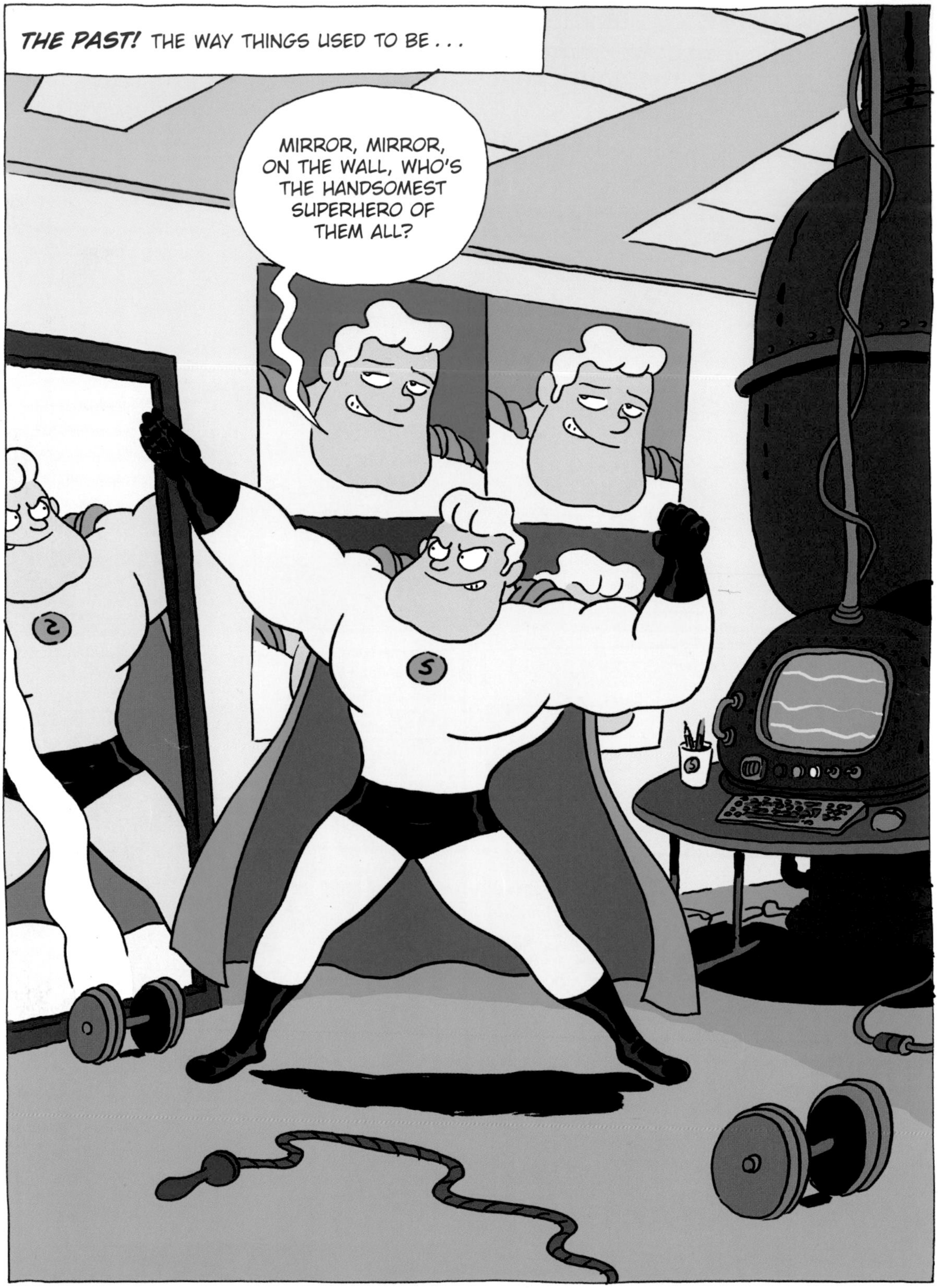
THE PAST! THE WAY THINGS USED TO BE . . .
MIRROR, MIRROR, ON THE WALL, WHO'S THE HANDSOMEST SUPERHERO OF THEM ALL?

HUH!?
AAHHH . . .
PLOP
WHAT A DISGUSTING BUG!
UGHHHHH!
WHO SENT YOU?
PRINCESS SKELETON? ZOLTAN THE DARK?
SUPER MAX HAS A LONG ENEMIES LIST.
WHEW.

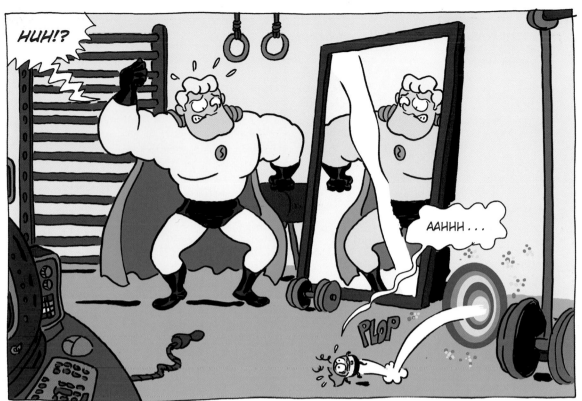

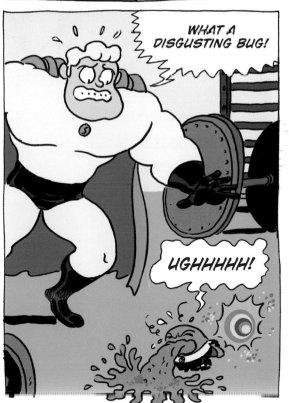

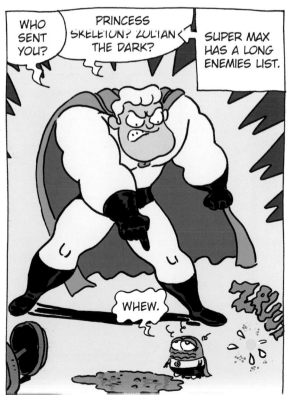

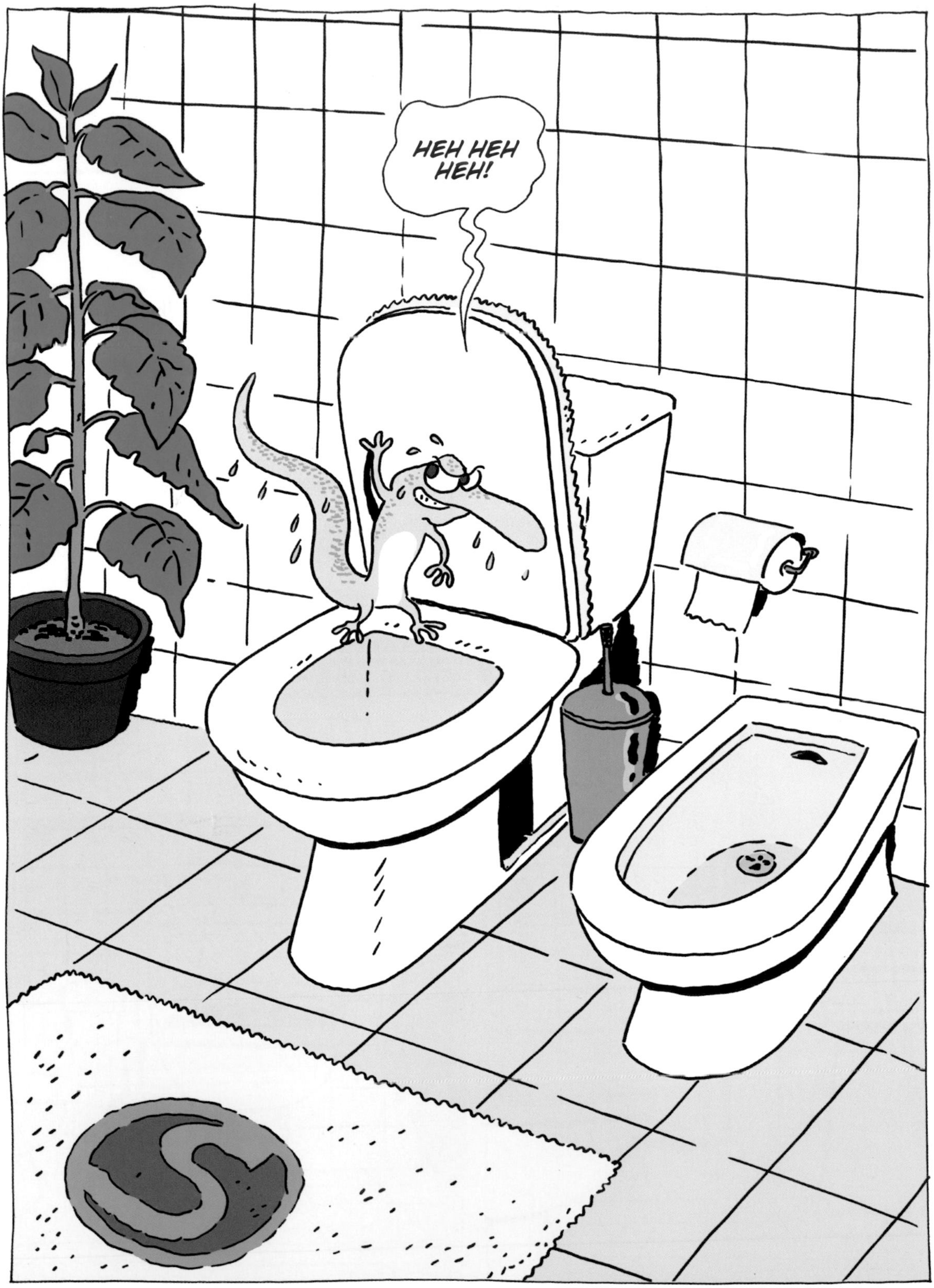
HEH HEH HEH!

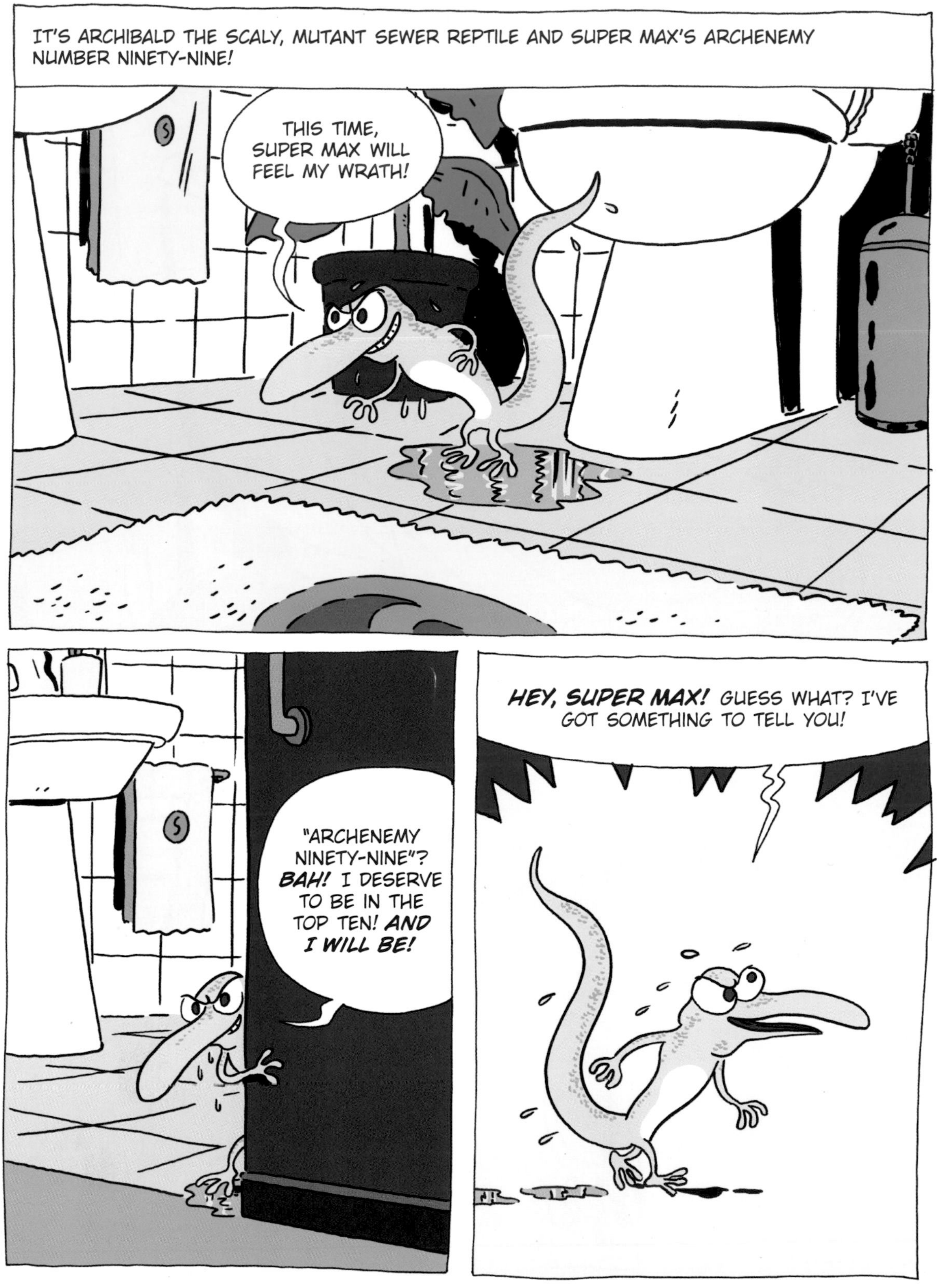
IT'S ARCHIBALD THE SCALY, MUTANT SEWER REPTILE AND SUPER MAX'S ARCHENEMY NUMBER NINETY-NINE!
THIS TIME, SUPER MAX WILL FEEL MY WRATH!
"ARCHENEMY NINETY-NINE"? BAH! I DESERVE TO BE IN THE TOP TEN! AND I WILL BE!
HEY, SUPER MAX! GUESS WHAT? I'VE GOT SOMETHING TO TELL YOU!

23

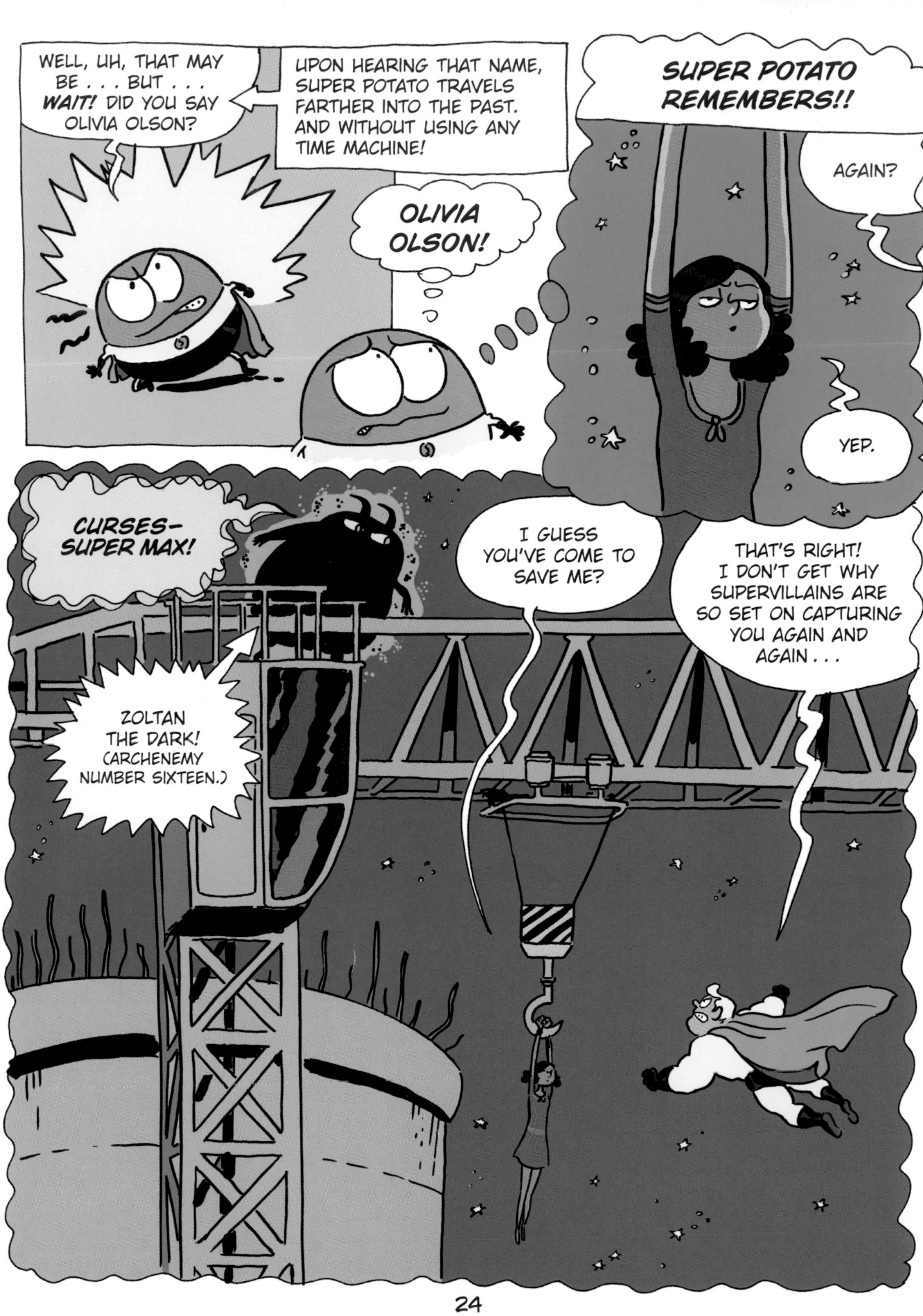
WELL, UH, THAT MAY BE . . . BUT . . . *WAIT!* DID YOU SAY OLIVIA OLSON?
UPON HEARING THAT NAME, SUPER POTATO TRAVELS FARTHER INTO THE PAST. AND WITHOUT USING ANY TIME MACHINE!
OLIVIA OLSON!
SUPER POTATO REMEMBERS!!
AGAIN?
YEP.
CURSES—SUPER MAX!
ZOLTAN THE DARK! (ARCHENEMY NUMBER SIXTEEN.)
I GUESS YOU'VE COME TO SAVE ME?
THAT'S RIGHT! I DON'T GET WHY SUPERVILLAINS ARE SO SET ON CAPTURING YOU AGAIN AND AGAIN . . .

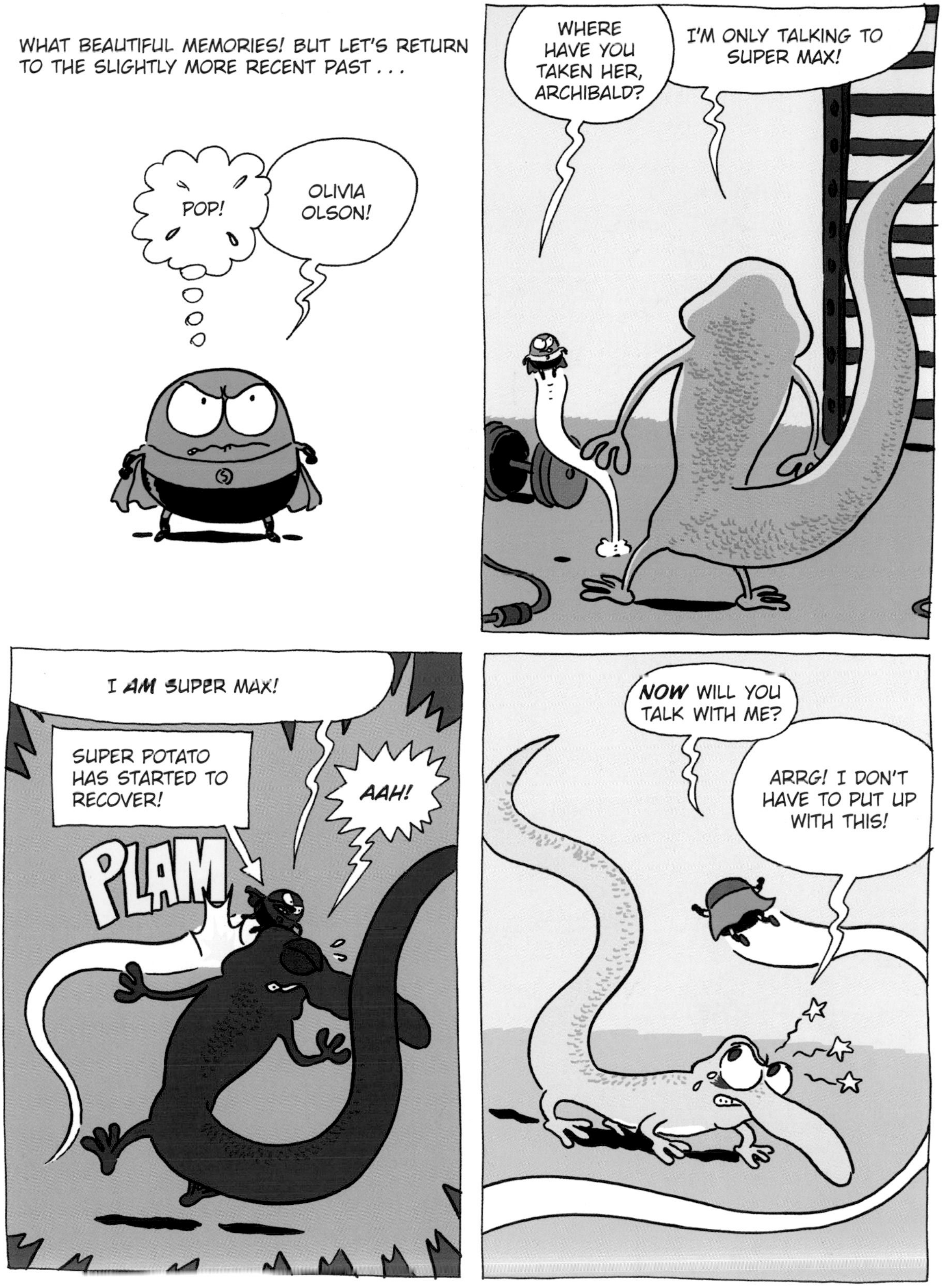
WHAT BEAUTIFUL MEMORIES! BUT LET'S RETURN TO THE SLIGHTLY MORE RECENT PAST . . .
POP!
OLIVIA OLSON!
WHERE HAVE YOU TAKEN HER, ARCHIBALD?
I'M ONLY TALKING TO SUPER MAX!
I AM SUPER MAX!
SUPER POTATO HAS STARTED TO RECOVER!
AAH!
PLAM
NOW WILL YOU TALK WITH ME?
ARRG! I DON'T HAVE TO PUT UP WITH THIS!

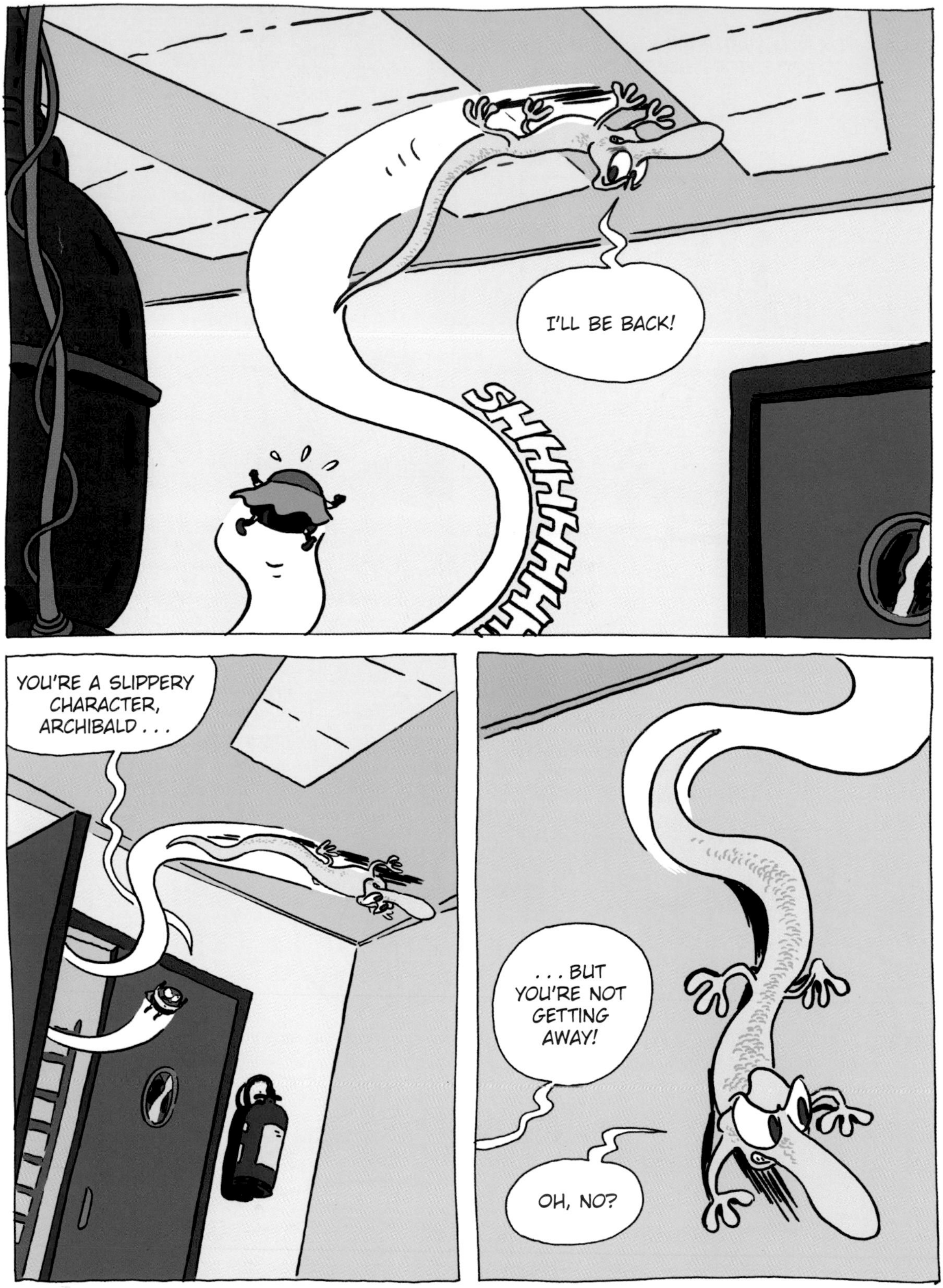
I'LL BE BACK!
SHHHHHHHHH
YOU'RE A SLIPPERY CHARACTER, ARCHIBALD . . .
. . . BUT YOU'RE NOT GETTING AWAY!
OH, NO?

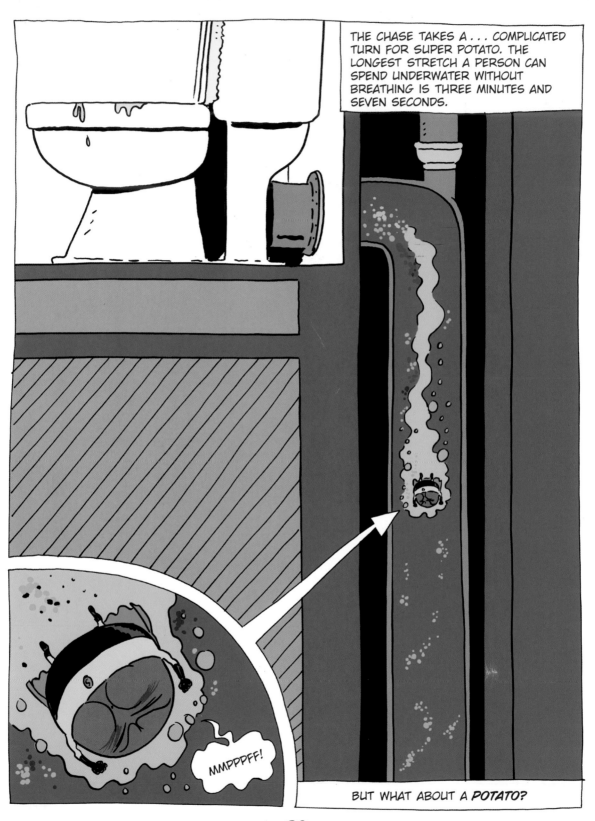

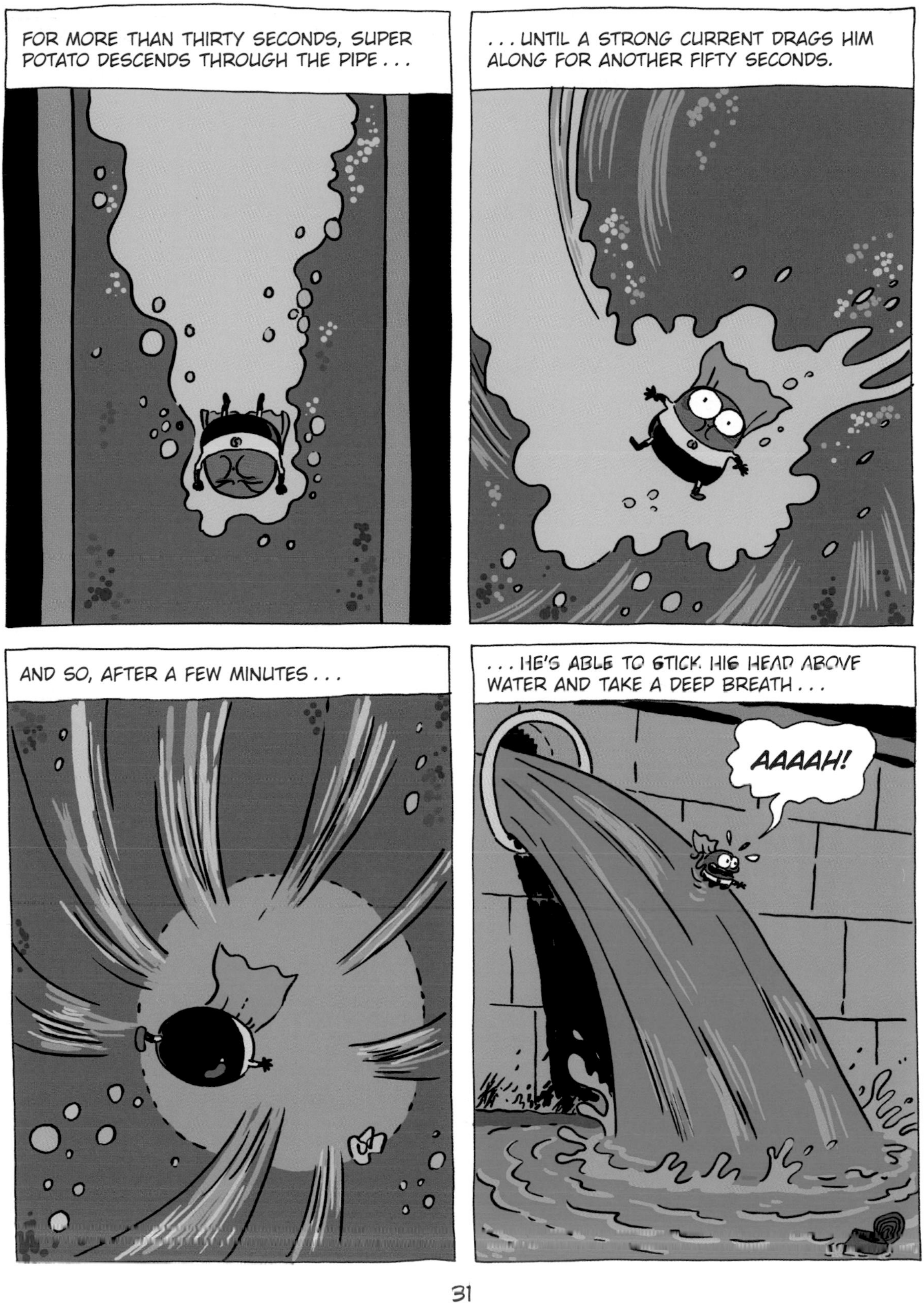
FOR MORE THAN THIRTY SECONDS, SUPER POTATO DESCENDS THROUGH THE PIPE . . .
. . . UNTIL A STRONG CURRENT DRAGS HIM ALONG FOR ANOTHER FIFTY SECONDS.
AND SO, AFTER A FEW MINUTES . . .
. . . HE'S ABLE TO STICK HIS HEAD ABOVE WATER AND TAKE A DEEP BREATH . . .
AAAAH!

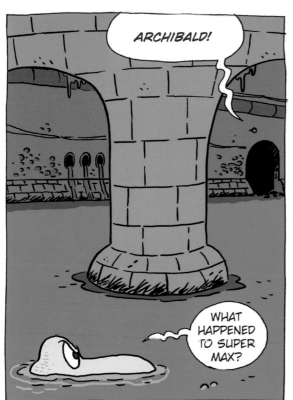

THEEESE TUNNELS HOLLLD NOOOO SECRETS FOR MEEEE. I'VE BEEN HERE LONNNGER THAN ANNNYONNNNE CAN REEEMEMBERRRRR.

PERRRHAPSS I CAN HELLLLP YOOUUUU, BUUUUUT . . .

. . . OOOONLY AFFTER YOOUUU SOLLLLVE THREEEE RIDDDDLESSSSSS.

THREE RIDDLES?

TO BE HONEST, I JUST WANT TO FIND ARCHIBALD THE SCALY. DO YOU KNOW HIM?

37

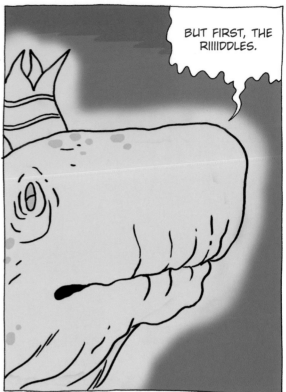

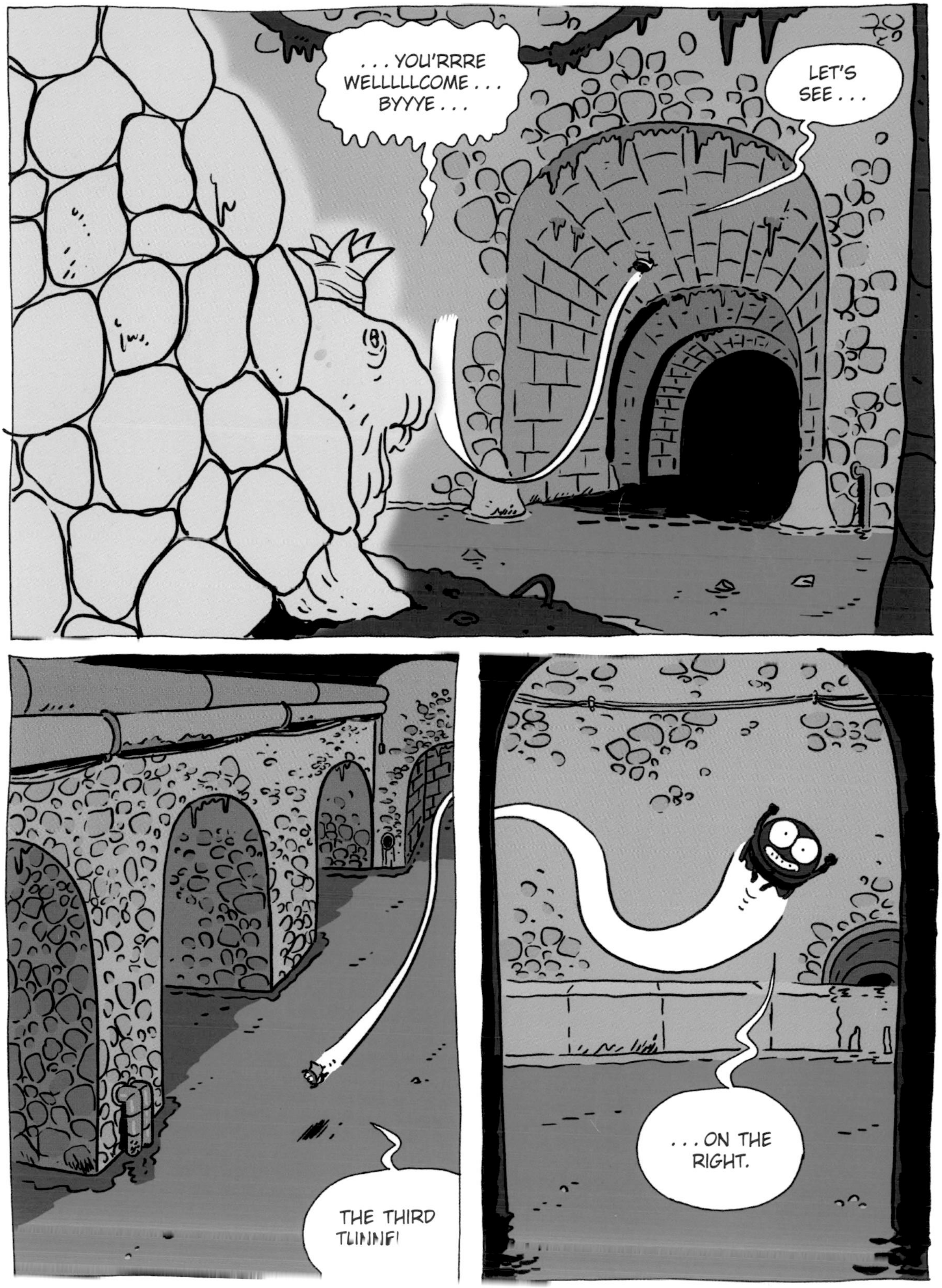
. . . YOU'RRRE WELLLLLLCOME . . . BYYYE . . .
LET'S SEE . . .
THE THIRD
. . . ON THE RIGHT.

44

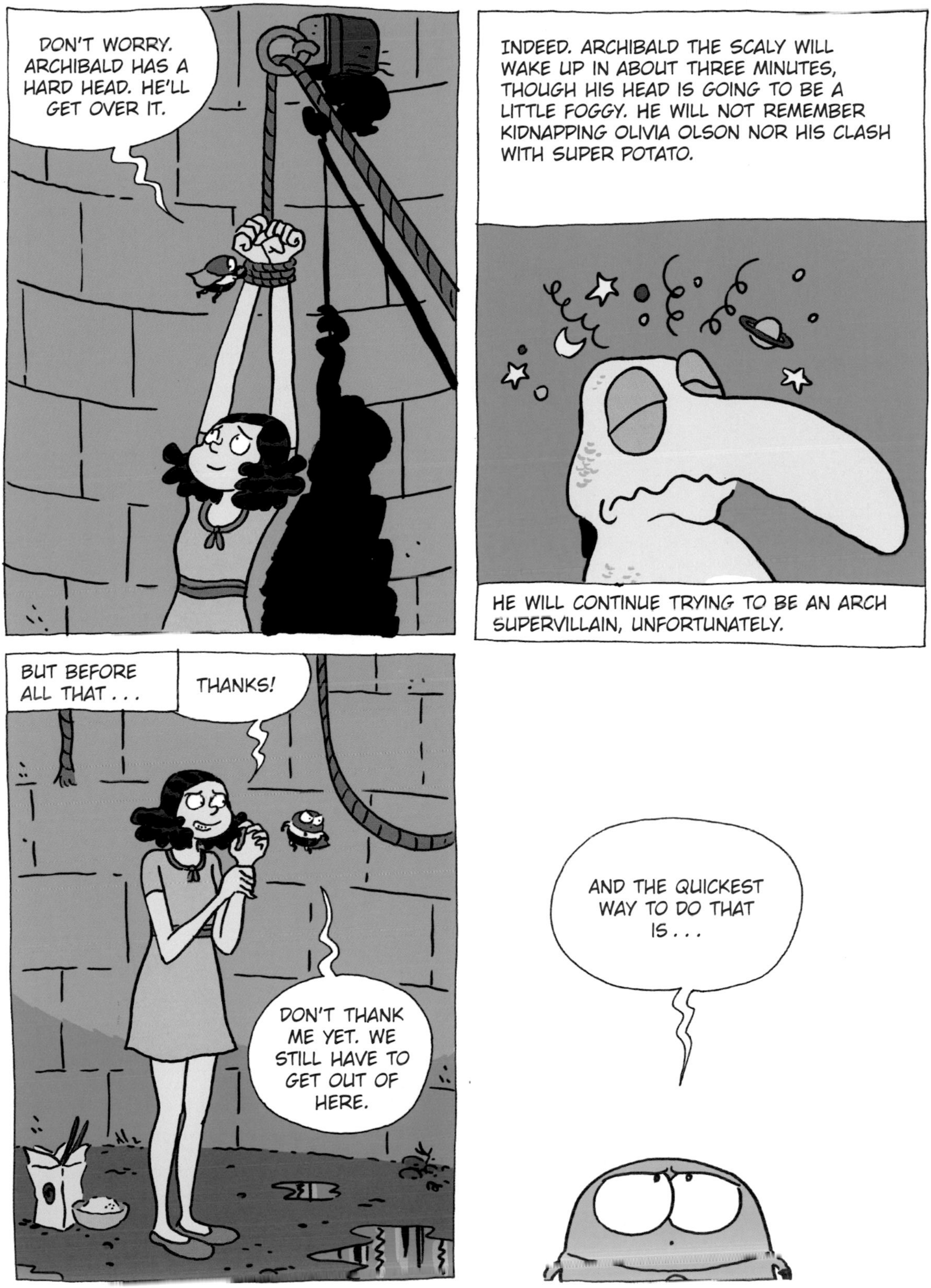
DON'T WORRY. ARCHIBALD HAS A HARD HEAD. HE'LL GET OVER IT.
INDEED. ARCHIBALD THE SCALY WILL WAKE UP IN ABOUT THREE MINUTES, THOUGH HIS HEAD IS GOING TO BE A LITTLE FOGGY. HE WILL NOT REMEMBER KIDNAPPING OLIVIA OLSON NOR HIS CLASH WITH SUPER POTATO.
HE WILL CONTINUE TRYING TO BE AN ARCH SUPERVILLAIN, UNFORTUNATELY.
BUT BEFORE ALL THAT . . .
THANKS!
DON'T THANK ME YET. WE STILL HAVE TO GET OUT OF HERE.
AND THE QUICKEST WAY TO DO THAT IS . . .

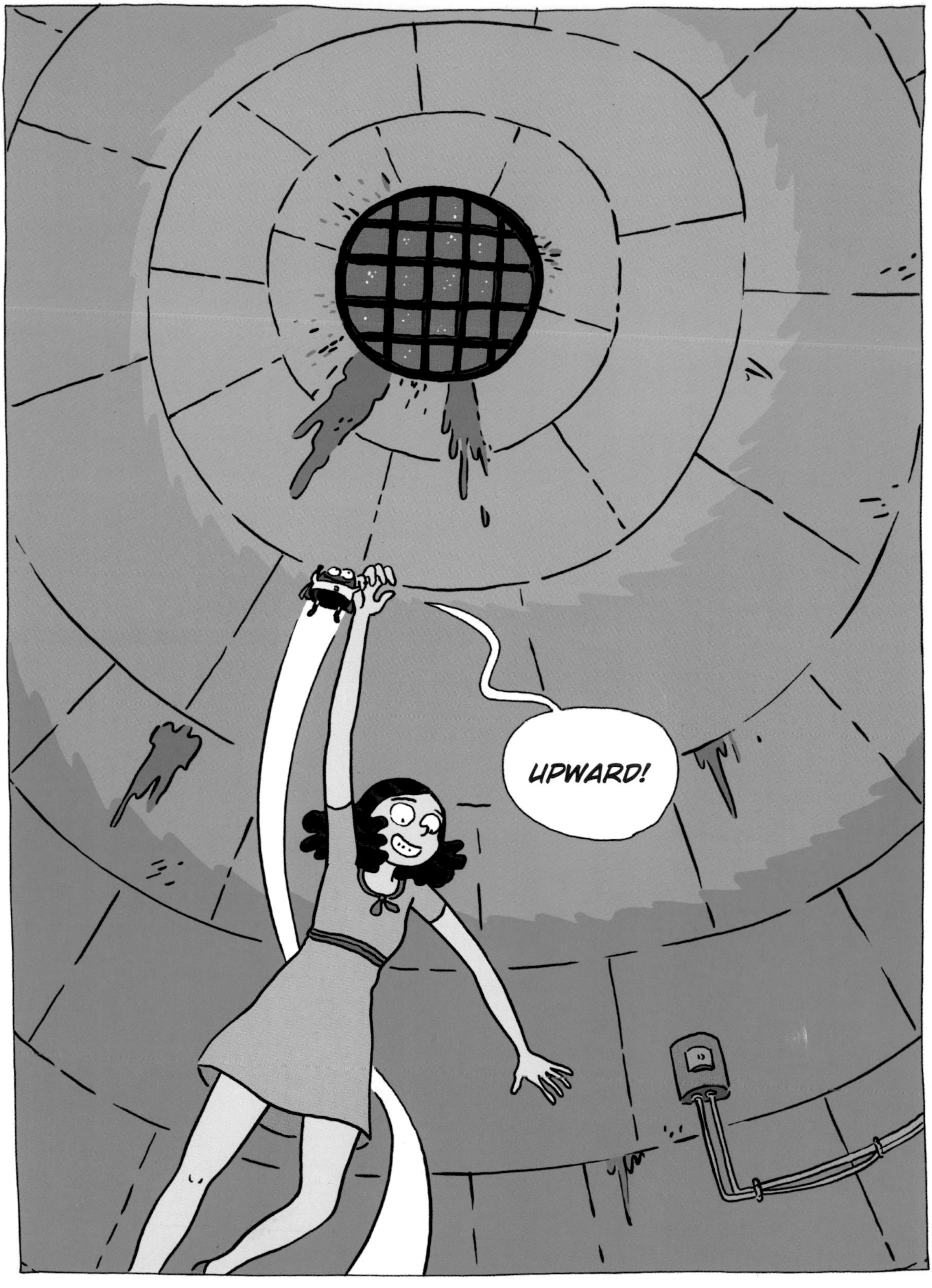
UPWARD!

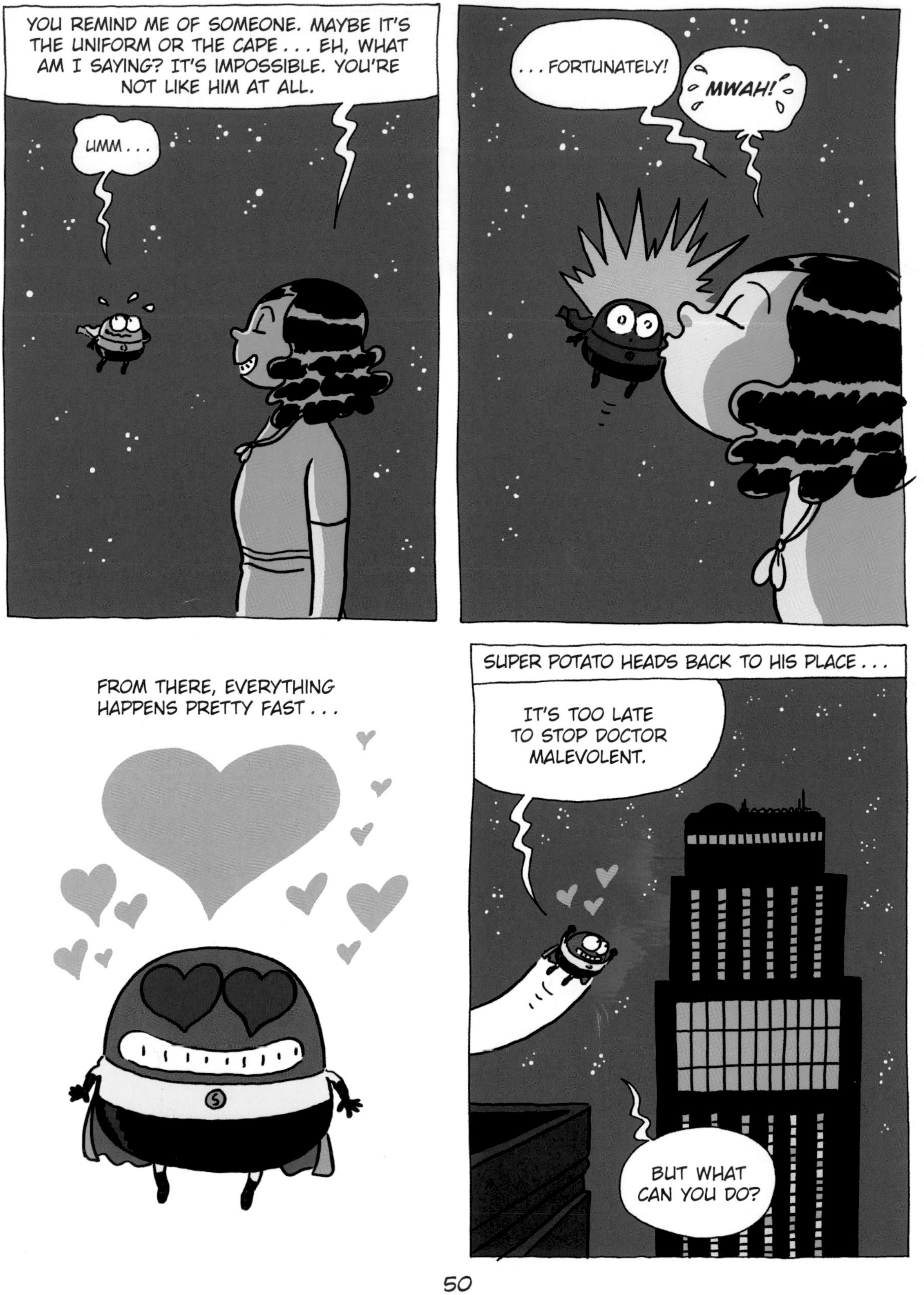
YOU REMIND ME OF SOMEONE. MAYBE IT'S THE UNIFORM OR THE CAPE . . . EH, WHAT AM I SAYING? IT'S IMPOSSIBLE. YOU'RE NOT LIKE HIM AT ALL.
UMM . . .
. . . FORTUNATELY!
MWAH!
FROM THERE, EVERYTHING HAPPENS PRETTY FAST . . .
SUPER POTATO HEADS BACK TO HIS PLACE . . .
IT'S TOO LATE TO STOP DOCTOR MALEVOLENT.
BUT WHAT CAN YOU DO?

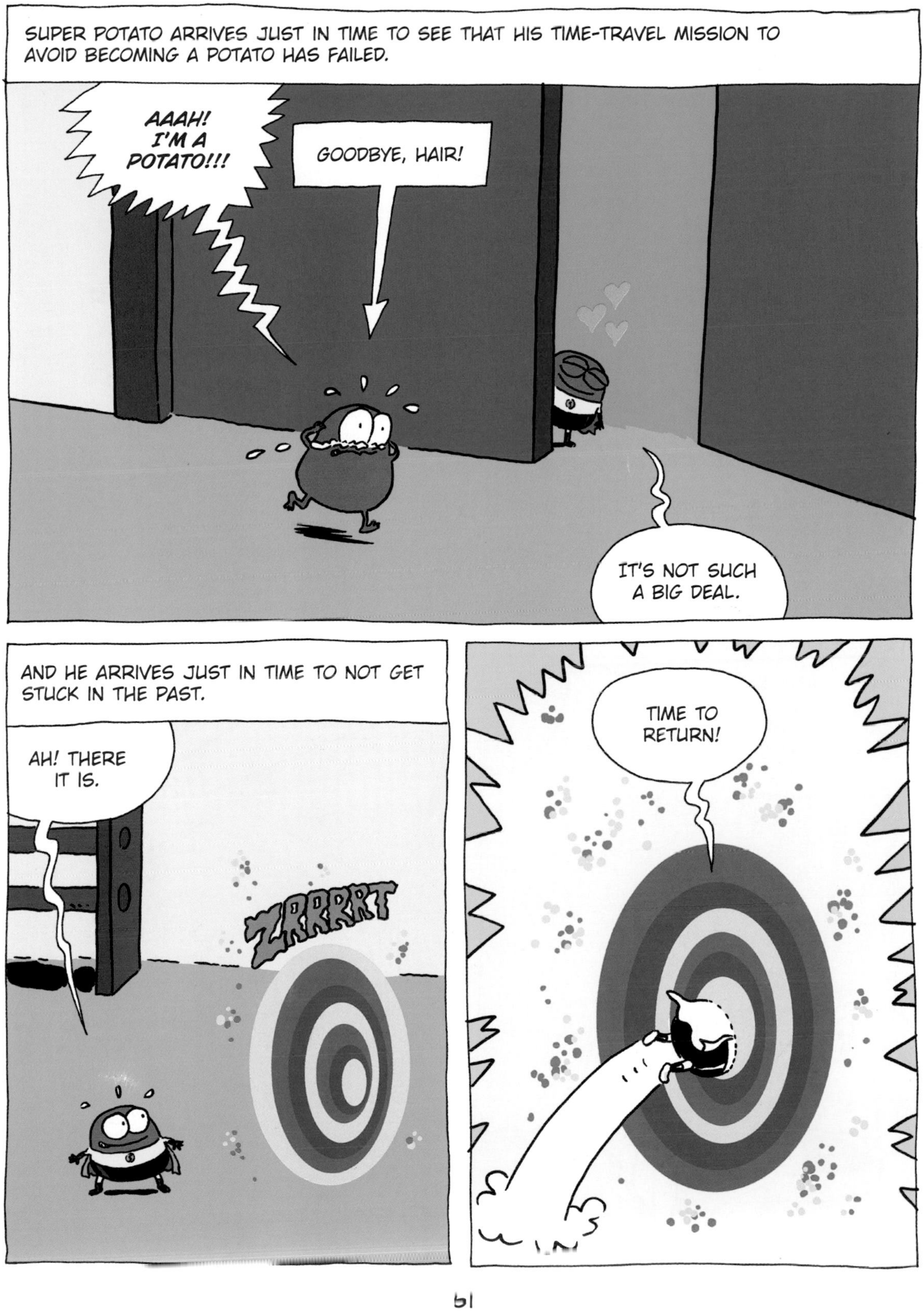
SUPER POTATO ARRIVES JUST IN TIME TO SEE THAT HIS TIME-TRAVEL MISSION TO AVOID BECOMING A POTATO HAS FAILED.
AAAH! I'M A POTATO!!!
GOODBYE, HAIR!
IT'S NOT SUCH A BIG DEAL.
AND HE ARRIVES JUST IN TIME TO NOT GET STUCK IN THE PAST.
AH! THERE IT IS.
ZRRRRT
TIME TO RETURN!

AAAAAAAH!!

IF MR. SUPER POTATO IS PUNCTUAL, HE SHOULD BE HERE IN... THREE... TWO... ONE...

ZERO!

AAAAH!

SUPER POTATO HAS ONLY DIPPED HIS TOES BACK INTO THE PRESENT WHEN...

...THE SMALL-TIME MACHINE EXPLODES!*

*THIS IS PROBABLY DUE TO A MANUFACTURING DEFECT.

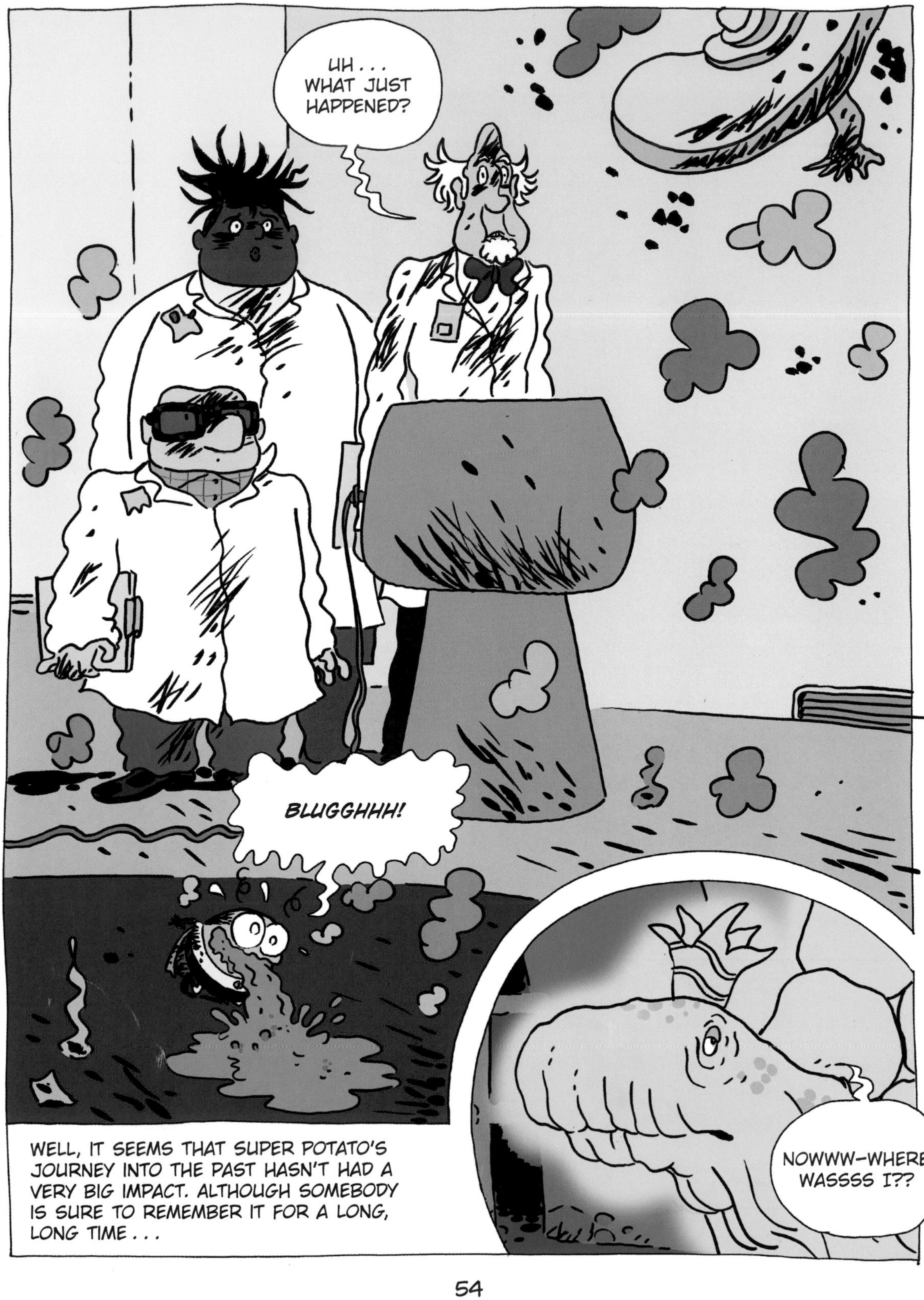
UH . . . WHAT JUST HAPPENED?
BLUGGHHH!
WELL, IT SEEMS THAT SUPER POTATO'S JOURNEY INTO THE PAST HASN'T HAD A VERY BIG IMPACT. ALTHOUGH SOMEBODY IS SURE TO REMEMBER IT FOR A LONG, LONG TIME . . .
NOWWW–WHERE WASSSS I??

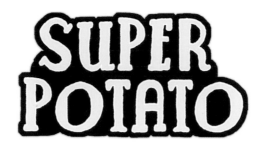

SUPER POTATO

Also available:

THE EPIC ORIGIN OF SUPER POTATO

SUPER POTATO'S GALACTIC BREAKOUT

SUPER POTATO
#1 THE EPIC ORIGIN OF SUPER POTATO
Artur Laperla
SUPER POTATO
#2 SUPER POTATO'S GALACTIC BREAKOUT
Artur Laperla

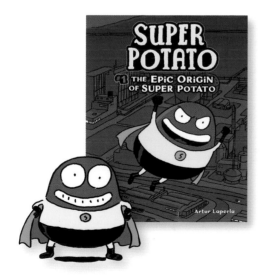

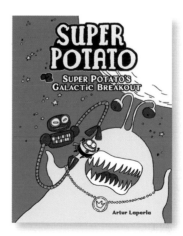

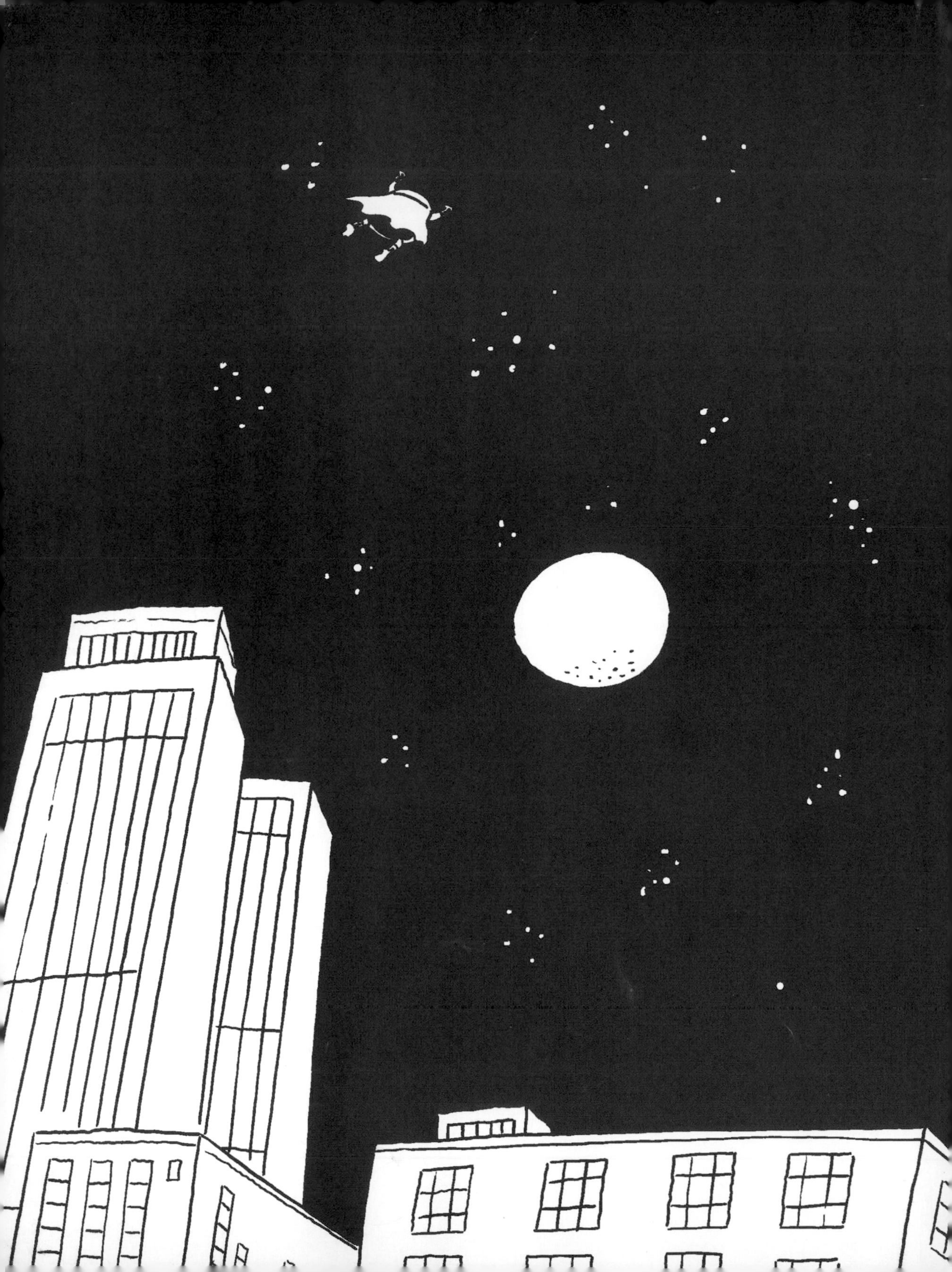